PRAISE FOR
IDENTITY THEFT

There are some of us Gentiles who love Jesus, love Jews, love Jesus as a Jew, and realize we were drawn into an Hebraic faith when we became Christians, and we have long hoped for better literature to serve our cause. Much that is written about Jesus as a Jew is a scolding distribution of blame rather than an ennobling call to truth. Ron Cantor has changed this. He uses fiction, humor, a bit of fantasy and a time traveler's imagination to tell us a tale that ought to be told. He makes us know Jesus anew. I am grateful; and I hope he is forerunner of a new tribe on the rise.

STEPHEN MANSFIELD
New York Times bestselling author

Ron Cantor is not only married to one of my favorite people on the planet, he is also a friend and co-laborer in Messiah for well over two decades. In his book, *Identity Theft,* you will find him witty and clever as well as insightful as he shares Jewish roots from a totally unexpected angle. I was pleased to discover that *Identity Theft* is an engaging page-turner! I believe you will find this book to be pointed as well as helpful, and you might even catch yourself becoming an agent in restoring Messiah's true identity!

PAUL WILBUR
Recording artist
Integrity Music

Ron had my rapt attention from page one of the Introduction! And what a great title, as Ron effectively portrays the identity theft of the centuries—that Jesus has been robbed of His Jewishness! Tragically, many of those who professed to believe in Him would have put Him in the gas ovens of Europe had He lived during their lifetime.

DON FINTO
Author, *Your People Shall Be My People*
Former senior pastor, Belmont Church
Nashville, Tennessee

Ron Cantor's new book, *Identity Theft*, is as riveting as it is revelatory and as entertaining as it is enlightening. With the unique vantage point of a Messianic Jew living in Israel, Ron gives you a guided tour of history from the pages of the New Testament to the Holocaust and then back to the Cross for an extraordinarily powerful portrayal of the Messiah's sacrificial death. Buy a copy for yourself and one for a friend!

DR. MICHAEL L. BROWN
President, Fire School of Ministry
Concord, North Carolina
Host, national radio talk show, *Line of Fire*
Author, *Answering Jewish Objections to Jesus* series

I've known Ron for a number of years and have always enjoyed his ministry. When I read *Identity Theft* I was captivated by the story. I couldn't stop reading until I was finished. What a must-read for anyone wanting to be part of an incredible journey to faith in the Messiah!

DR. EVON G. HORTON
Senior Pastor, Brownsville Assembly
Pensacola, Florida

How ingenious to embed a powerful teaching in an engrossing novel of a Jewish man's search for the truth! Many Christians today are experiencing a longing to know more about their Jewish roots, which are so foundational to all followers of the Messiah. But to really understand Christianity's Jewish heritage together with today's Jewish culture and mindset, Christians must know both the biblical narrative and the story of the Jewish people over the past 2,000 years, as well as how it has been so influenced and even dominated by the Church. In *Identity Theft*, Messianic communicator Ron Cantor has written the book that will give you this information in unforgettable portraits from first-century Jewish believers to the tragic wanderings of the Jewish people up until today.

ARI AND SHIRA SORKO-RAM
Founders, Maoz Israel (www.MaozIsrael.org)
Senior leaders, Tiferet Yeshua Congregation
Tel Aviv, Israel

Not just dramatic, but exhilarating! An easy-to-read story that draws non-Jewish readers into Jewish consciousness and Jewish readers into Jesus's consciousness. While many novels distract people from life, this one contains a life-changing message that can transform a reader's life. Happy to recommend.

DR. JEFFREY L. SEIF
Chair of the Jewish Studies Department
Christ for the Nations Institute
Dallas, Texas

This much-needed work is important for all seekers of truth. Though I am not much of a fiction reader, I quickly found myself engrossed in Ron's manuscript and unable to put it down. *Identity Theft* is a great book for both those who recognize the Jewishness of our Messiah as well as those who've never truly considered His identity. As we enter into a season of unparalleled anti-Semitism, we must remember that our Messiah was born into a Jewish home, lived as a Torah-observant Jew, died as King of the Jews, and is returning as the "Lion of the Tribe of Judah."

SCOTT VOLK

Pastor, Fire Church

Charlotte, North Carolina

President, Hineni International Ministries

I first met Ron Cantor in our local congregation in Washington, DC, decades ago. It seemed readily apparent he would emerge in a leadership role, and this has happened. Now we serve together in Maoz Ministries (Israel), where he is the winsome televised messenger of God's good news of the Messiah.

His recent book, *Identity Theft*, artfully explains the ancient schism between Jews and Christianity. This he does not through dry theology, but rather through a captivating novel.

The book will fascinate both the Jewish and Gentile reader with its portrayal of the heartbreaking truth of the Church's treatment of God's ancient people. The robbing of Yeshua (Jesus) of His cultural identity has resulted in a terrible and lengthy tragedy to the Jewish people. Ron's book seeks to restore to Yeshua His original ethnic context. The story helps us to better understand and reveals many, many things.

PAUL LIBERMAN

President, Messianic Jewish Alliance of America

Publisher, *The Messianic Times*

Ron Cantor has written a fast-paced novel that power-fully defends the faith. It reflects the understanding of many Messianic Jewish leaders in Israel and speaks the Gospel with simplicity and clarity to Jewish people who do not yet follow Yeshua. This book will open up minds and hearts—not only for Jewish people, but for many in the Church who will be enlightened as they see the first followers of Yeshua in their historical Jewish context.

Dr. Daniel C. Juster

Executive Director, Tikkun International

President, Messianic Jewish Bible Institute

Jerusalem

Ron Cantor adds his voice to the still small choir singing out the truth of the story of Jesus, His Jewish life and times, and the tragic opposite effect the rewritten story has had upon the Jewish people and Christians. As an orthodox Jew, I have not been convinced by this book to change my own life, but I hope Ron is not "preaching to the choir," and Christians who feel uncomfortable with their understanding of Jesus will pick up this volume and discover biblical truths that they never knew existed. *Identity Theft* is an important milestone in the journey that Christians must take in times such as these, and by extension, it impacts Christian-Jewish relations as well.

Gidon Ariel

Christian-Jewish friendship cultivator

Founder of the Facebook group "Jews Who Love Christians Who Love Jews (and the Christians Who Love Them)"

and www.root-source.com

From the time I picked it up, I didn't want to put it down. Ron Cantor has ventured into "no-man's land." Is it possible that the bridge between Judaism and Christianity is where truth resides? This book will challenge Christians to reexamine their theological presuppositions and take a much different view of the origins of their faith. It will also challenge the Jewish community to reexamine their 2,000-year-old wound inflicted by Gentile hypocrisy and take a new look at this "Yeshua of Nazareth" in His real clothing!

RICHARD FREEMAN
Messianic Rabbi, Beth Messiah Congregation
Houston, Texas

Ron is a passionate communicator, teacher, and storyteller. I had the joy of serving with Ron in both Ukraine and Hungary where his teachings on Jewish roots, history, and Messianic theology blessed many. In this creative book, Ron takes you on a journey of his Jewish people's experience through the centuries. You will be enlightened and encouraged as you see the "family story" told in a very new way. I wholeheartedly recommend this book.

WAYNE WILKS JR., PH.D.
International Director, Messianic Jewish Bible Institute

If Jesus is both 100 percent deity and 100 percent human then it's essential to understand what kind of human He is. He is certainly not a blue-eyed Scandinavian as some have portrayed Him. For more than a decade, Ron Cantor has been passionately revealing the true face of Jesus to Israel and the nations. As Ron shows how Jesus came to earth as a Jew, many truths in Scripture become more comprehensible and alive. You'll be enriched by Ron's insights.

WAYNE HILSDEN
Senior pastor, King of Kings Community
Jerusalem, Israel

The emotional depth and immediacy evoked in this novel would be impossible in a theological tome with the same purpose. It's a book you will want to read at one sitting, and if you're like me, your only regret will be having to wait for the remaining two volumes of the trilogy.

Dr. David H. Stern
Translator, *The Complete Jewish Bible*

IDENTITY THEFT

IDENTITY THEFT

RON CANTOR

DESTINY IMAGE® PUBLISHERS, INC.
P.O. Box 310, Shippensburg, PA 17257-0310
"Promoting Inspired Lives."

This book and all other Destiny Image, Revival Press, MercyPlace, Fresh Bread, Destiny Image Fiction, and Treasure House books are available at Christian bookstores and distributors worldwide.

For a U.S. bookstore nearest you, call 1-800-722-6774.
For more information on foreign distributors, call 717-532-3040.
Reach us on the Internet: www.destinyimage.com.

ISBN 13 TP: 978-07684-4217-5
ISBN 13 Ebook: 978-0-7684-8606-3

For Worldwide Distribution, Printed in the U.S.A.
5 6 7 8 / 17 16 15

DEDICATION

This book is dedicated to all the indirect victims of this *Identity Theft*—the lost sheep of the house of Israel. I implore you to take a fresh and honest look at Yeshua (Jesus) the Jew.

I think you will be surprised.

In defending myself against the Jews,
I am acting for the Lord. The only
difference between the church and
me is that I am finishing the job.
—ADOLF HITLER

Chapter One

THE VISITATION

It happened a year ago. He came in a vision. I have never fully shared this with anyone, except my wife, and at first, she didn't believe me, but I felt it was time to put my testimony on paper.

After all, I am a writer and He chose to send His messenger to me. People must know the truth. Christians must know the truth. And by all means, Jews must know the whole story.

Is that it?

Three words that turned my life upside down: "Is that it?" It wasn't that I was unfulfilled. On the contrary, I was extremely content. I was five years married and had two amazingly cute little girls. At twenty-eight, with only a bachelor's degree, I had risen in the ranks. I already had a daily column in the *Philadelphia Inquirer* and a well-read blog. Life was perfect.

And yet *that* was the problem—what if there was something I was missing? Maybe there was a God out there who expected something from me. Maybe not, but the truth is, *I had no idea.* What keeps my heart ticking day after day? Who makes sure that it continues to pump blood through my veins?

I had taken all of this for granted. It suddenly hit me that we spend entire lifetimes working and planning just to make sure we are comfortable when we retire, which is a very short period of time. Yet we rarely consider what happens after retirement when we die. Is that it? Six feet under and never another conscious thought? Or is there life beyond the grave? And if so, where would I spend eternity? I had no idea.

I was determined to find God. I was full of questions and I had no clue where to begin. How do you *find God?* It's not like I could just Google Him as I had learned to do for everything else.

Where to start?

Being Jewish, I began to go to synagogue and even attend afternoon prayers, the Mincha service, when I could. It felt great when nine men were waiting and I showed up to complete the *minyan* (a quorum of ten Jewish bar Mitzvah'd males required to begin the prayer service). As a last resort they might grab some poor just-over-thirteen-year-old out of his studies to reach the required number, but then I would show up, saving the day.

While that made me feel good about myself, I didn't sense any personal connection with the Almighty. It was more a satisfaction that I had performed some religious duty, than actually feeling His presence. I began to study other religions and actually began to pray—not in a formal sense like in the synagogue, but I simply asked God to show me if He was real and what He expected from me.

To be honest, I was drawn to Jesus. His message of salvation was so different from any other religion I had studied. Every single one of them put the emphasis on what I did. *Do this on Friday. Do that in the morning. Be a good person. And by all means, never do this.*

But the message Jesus preached conceded that my case was hopeless. There was nothing I could do to please God in light of all I had done against Him. That was why He came; in order to give His life as a sacrifice; to take my punishment—or so they say. It was the only philosophy that didn't stress religious obligation, but instead presented me with the opportunity to accept the fact that 1) I was a sinner; 2) I could not save myself; 3) Jesus had taken my punishment; and 4) through faith in Him, I could have eternal life.

You may be thinking, *So what's the problem? Buy into it!* It's not quite so easy. You see, being Jewish, I was convinced that to believe in Him would be to deny my faith, my heritage, and my community. Everyone knew that to believe in Yeshua was to betray the Jewish people—a people who had suffered more than any other, and had so often suffered in the name of the very One to whom I was attracted.

Also add to that the fact that the whole Jewish community knew my father was the son of Holocaust survivors. Surely they would all turn on me. And it seemed to me that they would be right. What kind of a Jew takes sides with the descendants of the Crusaders? When I went to my rabbi to confide in him, he nearly bit my head off. He told me to drop my pursuit and never bring it up again—"For the sake of your family." I was completely and utterly confused and immobilized.

And then he came. His name is Ariel. I was at Starbucks sipping on double-shot espresso. I have never been a Venti, non-fat, no-foam, no-water, six pump, extra-hot, chai tea latte kind of a guy—just strong espresso. That was all I needed to get my creative juices flowing in order to write.

I was sitting there reading the paper, getting ready to start on my column, when suddenly the entire room became white. In fact, it was so bright that *white* seems like an understatement. Everyone was gone—the girl behind the counter, the tattooed hipster listening to his iPod, the student on his computer, the couple that appeared to be going over a business plan...*all gone!*

I was terrified. Suddenly a man appeared...*an angel*. He introduced himself. "I am Ariel, an angel of the Most High." He was about six feet tall, quite fit, with dark hair, dark skin, and a short beard. He was wearing a white robe, interestingly, just as I would have imagined an angel to be dressed.

I said nothing. "David, you who are highly esteemed, consider carefully the words I am about to speak to you and the lessons you will learn, and stand up, for I have now been sent to you."

When he said this to me, I stood up trembling.

"I have been sent to give you understanding. You are a confused Jewish young man, but you have found favor in the eyes of Adonai."

I knew Adonai was Hebrew for *Lord*. Even though I had not been very religious, going to Hebrew school three times a week during much of my teen years had not been a complete waste.

He continued, "I have come to take you on a journey, to show you the past, the present, and even the future. At times you will beg me to stop, but in order for you to understand the truth and help others to understand, you must experience it—you must experience *all* of it."

I found my voice, but could not think of anything to say. Before I knew it the angel grabbed my hand, and suddenly we were flying through time. It is very hard to explain on paper, in words, what I was experiencing, which is one reason that it has taken me a year to begin this testimony.

I somehow knew that we were going back in time. It was thrilling and yet petrifying. I could see scenes in time, but from a distance. And then everything suddenly grew bigger, as when a plane lands. As though watching a timeline, I could see that we were in the second century, and then the first. Things grew really close, as if we were zooming in on Google maps. The Middle East, Israel, Jerusalem! And then, we passed right through a roof and gently landed inside what seemed like an ancient synagogue from the second Temple period. Only there were several rows of seats, like in a modern movie theater, and a massive screen. Torches lit up the room, as it was night.

There were other angels there. Two were above me and there were two at every entrance. They said nothing and Ariel didn't even acknowledge them. It appeared they were standing guard. Then I thought, *Am I in some kind of danger?* It reminded me of the first time I visited Israel. The armed soldiers at the airport made me feel safe and deeply concerned at the same time. From what and whom were they were protecting me? And now the question that plagued my mind was, *What dangerous spiritual force is seeking to bring about my demise?*

"What is going on? Is this a dream?" Words finally found their way out of my mouth. I knew this couldn't really be happening and yet I was quite sure I was awake. The only thing missing was Morpheus offering me a blue pill or a red one.

"David, your journey will begin here. You will watch events in the lives of four Jews, all from different time periods during the past 2,000 years. You see, David, you are struggling with the idea of *being Jewish and believing in Yeshua*. You don't mind if we refer to Him by His Hebrew name, do you?"

It was more of a statement than a question. He continued, "You feel that to believe would be a betrayal. But that is only because you do not know that the Yeshua you imagine in your mind is not the Yeshua who walked the streets not too far from where we are right now."

"So, we are in Jerusalem?" I asked.

"The Old City, to be exact. The year is 35 CE, a time when the Messiah was understood in the context in which the Jewish prophets described Him. The multitudes who followed Him during this period were all Jews.

"Over the years, that has changed. His message has touched nearly every nation...and that is a good thing. However, in the process, the nature and identity of the Messiah has been tampered with, even altered, by those without the authority to do so. In short, there has been an insidious case of identity theft.

"Long before computer hackers and credit cards, the most destructive, most horrendous case of identity theft occurred, and the victim was the Messiah Himself! Today, we will uncover it, and then you, young man, will expose it to the world."

This was getting interesting!

"Sit down. Let's begin," instructed Ariel.

Feeling completely confused and utterly intrigued, I sat in what was the most amazingly comfortable chair I had ever sat in, immediately forgetting the burden that he had just placed upon me—"You will expose it to the world."

I waited to see what would come next. Ariel picked up a remote, pointed it toward the screen, and pressed a button. The torches in the room faded, until it was completely dark. The film began to play.

Chapter Two

LIVING WITH SHAME

Words emerged on the screen:

27 CE, Capernaum, Galilee

Then a woman appeared and began to talk, as if she were being interviewed:

"I am a Jewess and my claim to fame is that my story, wonderful in and of itself, was recorded—at least the most important part—for posterity, by not just one, but by *three* ancient writers!"

As she continued to talk, I watched her story unfold like a movie.

"My name is Chaya. I spent my childhood playing on the shores of the Sea of Galilee. And each evening my father would come home after a day of fishing, bringing fresh tilapia with him for dinner. Now I know that the smell of fish isn't everyone's favorite, but for me it conjures up precious memories of my hardworking father who loved and provided for his family. My mother worked hard as well, taking care of the home and her children, using all her ingenuity to feed and clothe us. But no matter how hard they worked, there was never enough after paying the crippling taxes imposed by the nation's Roman overlords.

"Like most Galileans, we longed for the day when the Messiah would come and free us from the tyranny of the Romans. Every Shabbat we would go to the synagogue, in the center of our village, to hear the Torah read and to pray. It was a constant reminder to us all that God had saved our people once before when we were slaves in Egypt—surely He could do it again, and the sooner the better.

"In my late teens, around the age when many of my friends were being given in marriage, I began to bleed heavily. I went to every doctor in the area but none of them could help me. For twelve years I suffered greatly. The deepest pain of all was the social stigma, the loneliness, and the knowledge that no one would take me in marriage with this condition. I had no friends, because everyone I came in contact with would become ritually unclean. I began to realize that even if I lived a long life, I would never know the joy of having children, of holding a baby in my arms, or hearing my children's laughter at play. It broke my heart.

"Along with being emotionally drained, I was physically weak and, to make matters even worse, I was now destitute. Because I was unclean, I could never enter a synagogue to hear the Scriptures read. Over the years I had spent all I had on doctors and medicines—all to no avail. If it weren't for the fear of the Almighty, I think I would have taken my own life. *Baruch HaShem* (Praise the Lord), I didn't!

"I was in my late twenties when I first heard of the Rabbi from Nazareth. He was trained as a carpenter, they said, but He spoke like an angel—like someone who truly knew God, not just knew *about Him*. He had recently come to live in Capernaum and was invited to read from the Torah in our synagogue.

"I remember it so clearly. People were truly amazed by His words. He didn't speak like the other rabbis or the priests. He spoke with such authority!

"He created quite a stir, and several of the young men from our village attached themselves to Him. In fact, a number of them had worked with my father on the fishing boats. Jacob and John, two brothers a few years younger than I, actually became part of His inner circle.

"Before long, stories began to circulate that He could heal the sick. Suddenly, for the first time in many years I felt hope stirring within me. Could He heal me? But how could I, a woman who could hardly walk the short distance to the market, ever get close to Yeshua?

"For days I thought about nothing else. I was desperate. If He were to heal me, I could live again, maybe get married, even have children—I could have a life! But the more I thought about it, the more impossible it became. How could I, as a woman in my unclean state, ever get anywhere near the Rabbi?

"Then one afternoon, I heard a commotion outside. Because I lived so near the city square, I went out to see what was happening. Quite a crowd had gathered and I was told that Yeshua was coming, that He was on His way to the house of Jairus, one of the leaders in our synagogue. Jairus's daughter had been very sick and over the past few days had taken a turn for the worse. Earlier that day I'd heard they feared she might die. Jairus, in desperation, had begged Yeshua to come to his house and pray for his daughter.

"When I finally got to the square, I saw the Rabbi surrounded by masses of people. My heart sank. I felt so drained. I had no energy at all. Twelve years of bleeding takes its toll. And then, suddenly, I felt a surge of strength, of determination. I had to try. I knew that if I could just touch the *tzitzit*, the fringes on His garment, I would be healed. I was sure of it. I had to touch Him.

"Caught up in the crowd, I began to push and fight my way through. I am sure many were surprised that poor, quiet little Chaya was suddenly aggressively pushing her way past them. But if any were offended, I didn't notice. After more than a decade of weakness and suffering, I really didn't care. I meant to reach Him at any cost.

"In Jewish culture it is forbidden for a woman to publicly touch a man, much less a man she is neither married to nor acquainted with! Moreover, the nature of my problem deemed me perpetually unclean according to biblical law, so that anyone or anything I touched would become unclean. And yet, I was compelled, driven in my soul, to go through with it.

"Finally, I could see Him in front of me. One final charge! And just then, I was flung to the ground. The crowd was so thick that I thought I would be trampled. A foot on my hand, a kick in the back...*No!* I jumped to my feet and pushed forward until I was within reach of the Rabbi.

"*This was it.* With all the strength I could muster, I lurched forward, just barely managing to graze the fringe of His *tallit* with my fingers. And as I did, I felt such power come into me. But it was more than power...it was pure, it was clean, it was *life!*

"I knew in that moment that I had been healed, but more than that, I had been changed, radically changed. My life would never be the same. No, it wasn't that I would now be desirable to a man. At that moment, everything else was irrelevant compared to the pure joy that was radiating within me. I had found more than a husband—I had found the God I had only known from stories and traditions. Now, through this Galilean Rabbi, I was in the presence of the Almighty.

"Of course, I had believed in the God of Israel all my life. I had always celebrated the Holy Days of Passover and Yom Kippur, the Day of Atonement, Sukkot, and Shavuot. And I had hoped that the Messiah would one day come. But never had I realized that Elohim could be this close—He could be felt and experienced. And without ever realizing that I hadn't known it before, I now knew that *He loved me.*

"As all this was happening inside of me, I suddenly realized that the Master had stopped walking. He turned and asked, 'Who touched Me?' It seemed like a ridiculous question when dozens of people were touching Him as they pressed in. His puzzled disciples said as much. Yet, ignoring them, He continued to look around.

"I knew He was referring to me and I was terrified. I wanted to run, and yet I wanted to be with Him forever. The way He said, 'Who touched Me?' made me feel like I had taken something without permission. I was scared, but still I went forward and fell at His feet and confessed that it was I.

"*What had I done?* Everyone was looking at me. Barely above a whisper, I told Him about my sickness and how I felt that if I could just touch Him I would be healed. And just like that, a huge smile appeared on His face as He took my hand and said, 'Daughter, your faith has healed you. Go in peace and be freed from your suffering.'

"Those words changed my life. He called me *daughter* and despite the fact that I was nearly as old as He, I don't know that I ever experienced more fatherly love than I did at that moment. In an instant I was transformed from being unclean and undesirable, to being a woman who was healed and highly favored by the Messiah Himself."

Now I was crying, weeping with joy for this woman. My daughters had always laughed at how easily I can cry during a movie. But this was the most moving thing I had ever seen! Hollywood could never compete with Heaven!

She continued.

"You might be wondering whatever happened to the daughter of Jairus. Sadly, she died before Yeshua was able to pray for her. Yet, the Master still went to Jairus's home. When He arrived, everyone was weeping and mourning 'Why all this commotion and wailing?' He asked. 'The child is not dead but asleep.'

"But though they laughed at Him, He was not dissuaded. He threw everyone out of the house and, taking the child by the hand, told her to get up. And she did! She was brought back from death! We could hardly believe it!

"From then on He traveled from village to village throughout Galilee, Samaria, and Judea preaching the 'good news of the kingdom,' healing all who were sick and casting out demons from those who were oppressed. Oh, what an amazing time it was!

"Yet, how abruptly it all ended—or so we thought. On the eve of Passover, just a couple of years later, He was betrayed and handed over to the Romans by some of our religious leaders. Many thought that once the Romans arrested Him, He would then lead a revolt against them. But before we knew it, contrary to all expectation, the Romans crucified Him—they nailed Him to a cruel Cross! Crucifixion was the most excruciating kind of death that existed.

"Along with a number of others, I had followed Him to Jerusalem. We were all devastated. We had had such high hopes. We thought that, like Moses, He would deliver us from our enemies. But instead they killed Him. I don't have words to describe. With John by her side supporting her, His distraught mother was in agony as she watched her precious son die a torturous death. This was not supposed to happen! He was our hope.

"However, incredibly, after several days, in the midst of our despair, word began to spread that the One we had watched die, was alive. And unbelievably, it was true! He had risen from the dead. Over a period of forty days, His disciples and hundreds of other people saw Him, including me! And then, while His followers watched, He, our Messiah, was taken up into Heaven.

"In accordance with His last instructions, 120 of us stayed in Jerusalem and waited for the promised Holy Spirit. For ten days we prayed and many fasted. Then on Shavuot, while seeking Him in one of the enclaves of the Temple courtyard, without warning, suddenly, there was the sound of a mighty rushing wind and the power of Elohim fell upon us.

"Shimon, from Capernaum, left the enclave, part of Solomon's Porch, where we had been praying and ventured into the Temple courtyard. Under the power of God's Spirit he began to speak boldly to the massive crowd of Jews who were at the Temple for Shavuot. They were already wondering what was happening after hearing the sound of the mighty wind. He proclaimed to them that the Messiah of Israel lives. I had never before seen him like that. It was hard to believe that this was the same fisherman who had worked with my father. Suddenly, he had stature and passion. His words were tangible—like arrows piercing the hearts of his hearers. The thousands gathered there in the Temple courts hung on his every word as he spoke with incredible confidence and astounding authority about eternal life and their need to repent. That day our number grew from 120 to several thousand.

"That was all of ten years ago. Tens of thousands of Jews have found peace through Yeshua, their Messiah, since that day. And yes, I did find a husband, and we now have four children, all of whom, except the baby of course, have placed their trust in the Messiah, much to our delight.

"The future is bright. We know that soon Yeshua will return and this time He will set up His kingdom on earth, but first we must spread His message to the rest of Israel and to the Jews scattered farther abroad.

"Oh, and let me tell you the latest development that has everyone talking. We recently heard the strangest news from

Shimon. He claimed that Elohim told him to go into the house of a Gentile, a Roman commander named Cornelius, and to preach there. This caused something of a commotion, as we Jews would never normally go into the house of a Gentile.[1] They are saying, however, that when Shimon arrived there was a huge crowd gathered. As he began to teach, the *Ruach Hakodesh*, the Spirit of God, fell upon the people there just as He did upon us at Shavuot, and they began to speak in tongues and praise Elohim!

"Shimon thought, *If the Spirit is falling upon them as He did on us, how can we stop them from being immersed in water?* Can you believe it? We are all amazed that Gentiles are now following the Jewish Messiah and are even being immersed in water! No one is going to believe this!"

The movie ended and the lights came on. I turned to Ariel and said, "I don't understand. Why was she surprised that Gentiles were believing in Jesus? Virtually the only people I know today who believe in Him are Gentiles!"

"Let us not run too far ahead. All will be clear soon enough. Now sit down again," he gently said, "intermission is over." The lights dimmed and once again, just as before, a date and place appeared on the screen.

Note

1. To be clear, the Torah does not forbid fellowship with non-Jews, but the Pharisees placed a huge emphasis on ritual purity. Because they could never be sure if a Gentile had come into contact with something or someone unclean, it was far easier just to decree that you could not go into the home of a Gentile; that way you would know that you were not ritually unclean.

Chapter Three

"HaShem, Where Are You?"

1099 CE, Jerusalem

This time I could hear a voice, but there was no one being interviewed that I could see. "I am a Jew, and I am thirteen. My family has lived in Jerusalem for generations, going all the way back to Yehoshua (Joshua) son of Nun. But that family line is coming to an end. My name is not important since I will be dead soon. The Crusaders, of whom we have been living in dread, have finally broken into the city. They have already killed scores of Muslim soldiers. We Jews, those of us who are still alive, have gathered in the great synagogue hoping against hope for mercy, but I can already smell the smoke. Soon, we will all be dead.

"We've heard stories of these Christians who have come from every corner of Europe all the way to Jerusalem. If the rumors are true, and we pray to God they are not, the Crusaders have pillaged and slaughtered whole Jewish communities all along their way. We were told they were coming to *liberate the Holy Land* from the *Muslim infidels.* And truth be told, the Muslims have not been too kind to the Christians here in Jerusalem. Churches have been destroyed and over the centuries Muslims have murdered scores of them. The Christians had apparently had enough. But what does that have to do with me? I am not a Muslim!

"Their religious leaders, we're told, have promised them that if they die in battle, all their sins will be forgiven and they'll go to Heaven[1]—because they are serving Jesus Christ. But *where will I go if I die today?* I'm scared.

"We have always gotten along with our Muslim overlords—at least in my lifetime. They haven't persecuted us. In fact, my father Isaac and my older brother Michael fought valiantly with the Muslims to protect Jerusalem. Those Muslims are now dead—slaughtered one after another by the Crusaders as they broke into the city.

"They arrived in early June and surrounded our walls. Jerusalem is an isolated city, barely protected by its ramparts and surrounded by mountainous deserts. Once they encompassed us, we knew it was only a matter of time before they would break through. We could get no food into the city and they poisoned our water supplies. In mid-June, as I was helping the fighters on the wall, we could see them, see their large banners with huge crosses on them. That is their symbol. It's painted on their shields and sewn onto their tunics.

"Finally, two days ago around midnight, just over a month after their arrival, they broke through our defenses and took the city. While some escaped, I don't think there is a single living Muslim left in Jerusalem. As soon as they stormed through the gates, the Christians began to kill everyone around them, indiscriminately—men, women, and children, Jews and Muslims alike. There was blood everywhere. Bodies are stacked one upon another wherever you look. I have never seen anything like it—so much death. The stench is unbearable. People begged, they pleaded for their lives, but the Crusaders showed no mercy. The last image their victims saw was the vivid cross worn by their killers. It was as if these men were possessed.

"Our family, along with about 1,000 other Jews, has taken refuge in the great synagogue. Actually, the Crusaders' leader, Godfrey de Bouillon, drove us in here. This de Bouillon, it is said, is hoping to kill every Jew because he is convinced that every Jew is responsible for the death of Jesus. I don't know much about the New Covenant, but I thought it was a book about love and forgiveness, not killing and murder. Did this Jesus go around butchering women and children as His so-called followers are doing? And what does a thirteen-year-old boy, just bar Mitzvah'd, have to do with the death of a Jew over 1,000 years ago?

"Not that it matters what I think. Death has invaded our city. Hope is all but gone. They are mercilessly cruel. They have already murdered thousands of Jews throughout the city in the past twenty-four hours. We are the only ones left.

"How could it be that less than a month ago I was celebrating my bar Mitzvah at the Western Wall of the Temple Mount? I never dreamt that I wouldn't see my fourteenth birthday.

Such a day it was, reading from the Torah and chanting the blessings. They told me I became a man that day. Little did I know how quickly that would be the truth. Instead of playing with my friends or helping my father in our shop, I was supplying arrows to fighters on the walls of Jerusalem, fighting for our lives and watching Crusader arrows fly back at us.

"We had heard the stories of what they did in Europe. At first this was considered purely a war against the Muslims. But in Europe, greed and bloodlust perverted their cause. They reasoned, 'Why wait until we get to Muslim territory, when there are Jews, *Christ-killers*, all throughout Europe?' I overheard horrific tales coming from my parents—stories of rape and slaughter, stories of Jews being offered protection for money and then being killed by the very ones they'd paid!

"Inside the synagogue, I huddle together with my sisters, younger brothers, and my parents. My older brother is dead. We were told he was killed yesterday, shortly after the Crusaders broke through. He was sixteen. Will I be next? I'm too young to die. What have we ever done to these people?

"I will never grow up, never marry or be a parent. Today the Crusaders will kill me.

"Smoke suddenly makes its presence felt. Both the smell and sight of sinister tendrils of grey smoke curling their way under the heavy locked doors relay the dire extremity of our situation.

"HaShem! God!

"Flames begin licking their way in through the barred windows. It is getting hotter. The godforsaken savages are going to burn us alive. Even over the screaming inside the synagogue, I can hear the Crusaders singing hymns to this Jesus

Christ. What kind of religion is this? They are burning us to death and they sing of love? They have slaughtered nearly every human being in the city and they rejoice to the smell of burning flesh?

"The people who are praying, now increase their supplication in fervency and volume. Others collapse in shock. All are in a state of panic. Some are screaming and beating on the door. Others seek to shelter their children from the smoke as most back away from the walls, which are becoming scorching hot. The flames are now clearly visible on every side. The realization that their families and little ones really are burning to death finally becomes an inescapable reality against a backdrop of voices singing *Christ, We Adore Thee!*

"Incredibly, as the flames wrap themselves around rafters, which are beginning to collapse, and the intensifying heat causes some, mercifully, to succumb to smoke suffocation, the sound of these murderous Crusaders singing hymns to their Jesus Christ escalates.

"Yet, they say this Jesus was a Jew.

"It's inconceivable! They are singing to a Jew while they burn us alive for being Jews!

"HaShem! Where are You?"

I was angry! "Ariel, how could this happen? This is so different from the first story. What changed? What happened to healing the sick and raising the dead to life? Now they are putting the living to death! Clearly Jesus is not telling them to murder in His name, for His cause! I don't understand."

"David, it gets worse," he put a comforting hand on my shoulder. "You will have to bear with not understanding for a bit longer. In time, all will be explained." Once more the lights went out.

Note

1. Religion hasn't changed much in the past thousand years. Al Qaeda, Hamas, and other Islamic fundamentalist groups have sweetened the pot by throwing in seventy-two virgins for suicide bombers who die in the "line of duty." Yet, they have only copied the manipulative tricks of the Roman Catholic Church. How easy it is to motivate a poor peasant to fight for you when you promise him Heaven. We know from history that many of the Crusaders raped, pillaged, and killed without mercy. And yet, Church leaders went outside of scriptural authority, guaranteeing these men a place with Yeshua.

Chapter Four

IMMERSION OR EXPULSION

1496 CE, Tangier, Morocco

A young man is sitting in a chair.

"My name is Christophe. At least that is my *baptized* name. I am a twenty-three-year-old Jewish man. Several years ago we had to make an extremely difficult decision as a family. The authorities told us that if we didn't convert to Catholicism and join the Church, we would have to leave Spain.

"We were Jews, but Spain was home. Many of my father's friends had already joined the Church and been baptized. For a while they secretly continued to be our friends, but then, one by one, we ceased to see them.

"Their children were not allowed to play with us anymore. It wasn't their fault. Now that they had left Judaism, the

Church forbade them to intermix with *non-converted Jews*—we were poison. The punishment, should they be caught, might well be death!

"For many, many months my father wrestled with this decision. While many of his friends had already joined the Church and been baptized, many others had chosen to pack their bags and leave for other countries, such as Morocco to the south. However, they had to leave almost everything behind. Property was sold for a fraction of its worth. Jewelry was traded for food. We heard reports that some of our friends had been robbed and even killed on the way to their new life. My father did not want this for our family.

"One evening, he sat us all down and explained that if we wanted to survive and maintain our current quality of life, we would have to play their game. He told us that we would be baptized as Catholics, but remain Jewish in our hearts. This is what many Jewish families had done.

"We knew, and our tormentors knew as well, that this had nothing to do with religion; it was about politics. Spain was seeking to unify the country under Roman Catholicism. In fact, virtually all *non-Catholics* were suffering the same fate as we were.

"When the day came, not only were we baptized, but my father had to read a public confession denouncing Judaism as a demonic religion. He promised never to celebrate any Jewish holiday or even associate with non-baptized Jews. We were told that if we ever returned to Judaism, *in any form*, we would face severe retribution from the Church. They could confiscate our property and expel us from Spain. Even death was on the table. This was one of the worst days of my life. I felt so sick and dirty. How could we have compromised to this extent, trading in our faith for acceptance?"

This was how I felt. Although no one in twenty-first century America was threatening me with expulsion, I knew, like Christophe, that to become a Christian was to deny who I was. He continued.

"We were called *Conversos*, new Christians, or the more derogatory title, *Marranos*—meaning 'pigs'! Despite giving an appearance of welcoming us into the Church, they did all they could to humiliate us. It was clear that we would never be permitted to be one of them and yet we couldn't be who we were. We were stuck somewhere in the middle of no-man's land.

"My father reminded us many times that we were still Jews and would always be Jews, but that we must be very careful. Everything had to be done in secret. Just a refusal to eat pork was considered sufficient reason to have a person arrested. We could trust no one, as the Church had its spies. Imagine that, a religious institution hiring people to spy on their subjects to ensure truly Catholic behavior. How could such a system claim to represent God? And how did they expect such coercion to spawn true devotion? Well, of course, they didn't. This was all about Spain, not about religious devotion.

"Outside the home we maintained the facade of being good Christians while inside the home we remained God-fearing Jews. We lived this way for many years and while I carried with me a permanent feeling of uneasy guilt, we were able to remain in Spain. All that came to a very abrupt end, however, when my father was finally arrested.

"A *friend* came by to greet us on the Sabbath. Candles had been lit to welcome in the day of rest. We thought this friend could be trusted. In fact, he was a spy. In the beginning we had been much more careful—*especially* on Friday nights. Spies were encouraged to poke around the homes of *Conversos* on *Erev Shabbat*, Friday evenings, hoping to catch someone honoring the Fourth Commandment. Lighting Shabbat candles, saying the Jewish blessings, and singing the songs I grew up singing on Erev Shabbat were forbidden under the threat of death.

"Tragically, we had grown careless; we'd relaxed our caution. Three days later they came for my father. He was arrested and brought before an inquisition. The Church then tortured him until he confessed to the wretched crime of lighting Sabbath candles.

"My father was given a choice. He could repent of his deceit and take a part in a *verguenza*—a 'shaming,' in which he would be stripped to the waist in freezing temperatures (it was winter). He would then be paraded through the streets, led by monks and mocked by the crowds, suffering countless other indignities all along the way. The other option was to be burned at the stake.

"We knew additional punishments would be imposed once my father accepted the *verguenza*. They would expect him to turn in other *Conversos* who were secretly living as Jews, but he had been humiliated enough. Hadn't he already denied his faith, in public, for our protection? And now these Christians wanted to add insult to injury. No, it was too much. He would not!

"When my father declared he would not recant, he was taken back into custody and sentenced by the religious magistrates, apparent followers of this Christ, to be burned alive.

Yes, my father would be tied to a stake and endure the inconceivable agony of burning to death as the fire slowly, painfully, consumed him.

"All this in the name of their religion!

"When the day came, my family watched. We did not want him to die alone. This was it. The *religious police* were going to kill my father—take him from me because we lit candles. They brought him out with his hands bound behind his back. He was tied to a stake. He said not a word. Even when the flames engulfed him, burning his living body, he would not scream. He was telling us, without words, *'Don't give in...don't compromise...be strong...'* and then, my father died.

"After my father was murdered and all our property confiscated, we did what we should have done in the first place. We made the journey to Gibraltar and sailed on to Morocco, where we settled into a thriving Jewish community in the city of Tangier. I miss my father deeply and I will never forget his courage. I live to honor his memory and to honor Judaism, for which he laid down his life.

"Oh, and by the way, please don't call me Christophe. My name is Jacob."

"Ariel, I can't handle much more of this. I studied the Inquisitions in college, but that was just words in a book. This is different. Those poor people! How could Christians act this way?"

"Patience, David, patience."

At this point, my mind had ceased trying to determine whether I was imagining all this or really talking to an angel and traveling through time. My emotions were fully gripped by what I had just seen. All that we Jews had ever wanted was the freedom to make a life for ourselves, but it seems there was always someone seeking to prevent that and to persecute us. I thought, *My God, Hitler didn't have to look too far back in history to find a pretext for killing Jews. He needed only to look at the Church.* And then it hit me.

"No Ariel! I can't! I won't watch it! Take me back! It's too much..."

Chapter Five

HORROR!

The lights dimmed, but this time I wouldn't watch. I sought to get up in order to escape and found that I couldn't. I was literally glued to my seat. I yanked and jerked, but nothing worked. I was stuck there. Finally I resigned myself. On the screen were the words:

1945 CE, Bergen-Belsen Concentration Camp

And a young boy began to tell his story of horror.

"My name is Tuvia Lebowitz. I am sixteen years old. Today, I am free. But while my body is free my soul will ever be captive to memories and horrors too painful to utter. My mother is dead. My father is dead. My sisters may be dead. My little brother is dead. And I have not eaten a proper meal in five years.

"It all began when I was ten years old. My father was a university professor. We lived a comfortable life and I was happy. My friends were Jewish and Polish, but over time fewer and fewer of my Polish friends were permitted to play with me. I was very sad about it and so were most of them. But one day one of those boys, Jacek, came up to me as I walked home from my violin lesson, and yelled, 'You Jew! You killed Christ. You will also suffer!'

"I had no idea what he was talking about, but the anger with which he said it sent a shiver up my spine like I had never known before. The coming years, however, would bring ample fulfillment of the premonition I felt in that moment.

"The day came when all the Jews of Warsaw, nearly a third of the city's population, were required to leave our homes and move inside an area that was smaller than two and a half percent of the city. Four hundred thousand people were living in an area that was designed for just over three thousand!

"Once inside, no one was permitted to leave the *ghetto*, as it came to be called, without a work permit. And these were restricted mainly to older people. Fortunately, my father was one of the few to be granted one, although his status as a university professor was now relegated to *factory worker*.

"Over time, food in the ghetto became scarce. We were surviving on fewer than 200 calories a day. My father would sell some of our possessions to keep us from starving. It wasn't uncommon to see dead bodies on the streets. Some starved, others froze to death, and some just gave up. Hunger and disease were the two biggest killers. There were, of course, those who told us this would all pass, that we had simply to obey the rules and in time all would return to normal. *They can't kill all of us*, they reasoned.

"The day came when we were informed that trains were to transfer us out of the overcrowded ghetto. We were told that families were to be resettled in better areas in the countryside. It was a welcomed prospect and I hoped that we would be among those selected to leave this dirty, congested place for the country. But then rumors began to trickle in that the families who were leaving were not going to a better place, but to concentration camps where some were killed and others were forced to work for the Nazis. Many simply refused to give credence to these stories while the rest of us were terrified. But again, our leaders assured us that these were just rumors and everything would soon be all right.

"And then our name was called—we would be going to the countryside. We took all our belongings, which weren't many, and boarded a train. There were no seats like on the trains I used to love to ride when we traveled from Warsaw to visit my grandparents in Lodz. *My grandparents*? What had become of them?

"We crowded into the cattle cars and just when I thought I had found a place to stand, I was shoved backward. The car was already full, but they just kept herding more and more people into the car. *Where was my little brother?*

"The heat was simply unbearable and almost immediately, the complaining began: *We are going to die in here. Move. I need more room. They might as well bury us in this train as we'll never survive.* I could hardly breathe, we were packed so tightly together. It was terrifying. After a few hours, people needed to relieve themselves and with no facilities, the stench was horrible. They had told us things would get better, but they only got worse. No one could have imagined that we'd be in that cattle car for four days without food or water. Sleep was nearly impossible, but after a couple of days you fell into a state of stupor where you could be asleep and awake at the same time. I would dream that I was back at home only to be jolted out of my fantasy, as someone would faint or cry out, returning me to this living nightmare.

"After three days, a woman standing just a few spaces from me collapsed. She was dead. She didn't appear to be much older than my mother, whose sobbing could barely be suppressed as my father sought to console her.

"I had just turned thirteen. I was supposed to have had my bar Mitzvah by now. I would have stood proudly in the synagogue, chanted from the Torah, and endured the praises of my family, friends, and relatives. Instead, here I was enduring suffering like I had never thought possible. How much more of this could we take?

"The next day we arrived at a work camp. We were taken off the train and separated into different groups. When my mother was told to follow the women, she became hysterical. She grabbed my little brother and begged the guards not to separate them. They ripped him from her and when she protested, the butt of a guard's rifle found the back of her head, knocking her to the ground. I was in shock. Was this really happening? I wanted to fight, but I couldn't move.

"And then, when it seemed things couldn't get any worse, one of the other guards solved the dilemma by pulling out his handgun and putting a bullet through Chaim's head, with as much emotion and effort as he might have used pouring himself a glass of water. My little brother lay dead on the ground, blood streaming from the gaping hole in his head. The image haunts me to this day, and always will.

"No one cried, no one screamed—we were simply in shock. Surely what we had just witnessed with our own eyes didn't really happen. Chaim couldn't be dead. And yet, he was. A five-year old Jewish life was of little consequence to the Nazis.

"Father and I were herded into the men's line, while my grief-dazed mother, still in shock, was pulled into another line. We would now work for our tormentors. My two sisters, barely twelve and fifteen at the time, were placed with other girls their age. Only later did I learn what would happen to these girls. They would be used to service the Nazis. Fortunately, I was too young to understand such things. It would have been too much for me. But now I am a man. I'm sixteen and know exactly what they did to my sisters. I don't even know if they are still alive.

"My mother only survived a few months. The devastation of watching her baby, her youngest son, murdered before her eyes, robbed her of the will to live. She was inconsolable. The other women covered for her as best they could, but soon it became clear to the guards that not only was she not doing her share of the work, she no longer cared whether she lived or died. Mercifully, before she could be sent to the gas chambers or terminated, she was gone. One morning she simply didn't wake up.

"This happened three months after we arrived, but my father and I only found out a year later. I didn't even weep. By that time I was completely numb. Death was everywhere.

It had become too familiar to warrant a response. I was sure it was only a matter of time before these monsters or this godforsaken place would kill me as well. My father, on the other hand, was completely undone by this news. He held on for another year, for my sake, but in the end, hopelessness, despair, and malnutrition claimed him. Like my mother, one morning he simply did not wake up.

"At fifteen I was, at best, the man of the house, or at worst, the only one left in the house. Part of me hoped my sisters were dead. The thought of some sleazy, overweight, Nazi officer with alcohol-laden breath, laying his hands on either one of them, sickened me.

"I was transferred to Auschwitz, a death camp, in early 1944. As I passed through a gate a guard hissed at me, '*You killed Jesus Christ; now we will kill you.*' Jacek was right. They blamed me for the death of a man who died 2,000 years ago—a Jew no less, someone they themselves would have killed, given the opportunity. I was fifteen; I had never killed anyone! And I wondered, in passing, what exactly had become of Jacek. For all I knew he could be living in our house. Or maybe he'd joined the Hitler Youth, and was now training to fight for the Nazis.

"The guards obviously agreed with Jacek as they forewarned us of our fate, their retribution for our crime of killing Christ. The butt of a rifle in my stomach accompanied the threat, in this instance. How much more could I take?

"They then moved us to Birkenau, one of the camps adjacent to Auschwitz. There in a red brick building, which from the outside appeared harmless enough, they had built fake shower blocks. Instead of encountering clean water, unsuspecting victims were led into the showers and asphyxiated by poisonous gas.

"This was one of the cruelest and yet most efficient tricks of the Nazis. How do you kill thousands of people at one time and keep them from panicking, or worse, revolting? You give them a cake of soap and tell them they are going to receive the first shower they have had in weeks, or months.

"The red brick building was just one of many such death machines. Its only distinction lay in the fact that it had been the first, or so I was told. I know this because it was my job to remove the bodies. Every day, all day, I dragged the lifeless corpses of my people out of the gas chambers, loading them onto carts to transport them to the crematoria, all the while hoping against hope that I wouldn't share their fate.

"I was surrounded by death. I no longer felt human, so I guess they'd won. Clearly that was the subliminal message the Nazis transmitted by transporting us in cattle cars. In truth, I felt just like an animal seeking to survive the barren winter— only winter was now going into its fourth year.

"Finally, in January 1945, the Germans began to demolish the gas chambers. Our captors blew them up, one by one. They seemed intent on getting rid of the evidence. You could see the fear in their eyes. Was this war coming to an end? Would we soon be free? Was someone coming to rescue us?

"Our hopes of freedom, however, were soon crushed. The barely living were rounded up and ordered to march from Auschwitz to God knows where. Thousands who were too weak were simply left behind. It was freezing, the dead of winter. Tens of thousands of us marched and marched. It was nothing for someone in front of you to simply collapse. Those who couldn't walk were left for dead. I passed hundreds of dead bodies. Who knows if they were dead when they hit the ground or simply froze in the snow? What would once have shocked me had become commonplace. A dead body, even that of child, barely fazed me. What had they done to me?

"I had determined from the outset that I would survive—if not for me, in the faint hope that I might one day see my sisters again.

"Finally, we arrived at Bergen-Belsen. By April, most of the guards had fled, but the remaining ones seemed perversely intent on leaving no inmate alive. After several days with no food or water, more and more Jews began to collapse, go crazy, or simply die. Bodies were everywhere. Typhus was spreading. Surely my body would soon succumb to these deathly conditions.

"And then, yesterday, April 15, 1945, five days after my sixteenth birthday, British troops arrived and—miracle of miracles—we were emancipated!

"Now I am free. Or so they tell me. What does that even mean at this point? My parents and little brother are dead. My sisters, if alive, have been violated repeatedly for years. *What will become of me*, of Tuvia Lebowitz?"

By now I was sobbing inconsolably.

"David," the angel called out. I didn't answer. "*David Lebowitz!*" he called out again.

Chapter Six

FROM CHAYA TO TUVIA... HOW DID WE GET HERE?

Still sobbing, I cried out, "But why?"

"I told you it would be hard, but He has a task for you, and you have to feel it deeply so that you can deliver it effectively, even though it pains you—even though you feel like your very guts are being ripped out."

I calmed down. "You know, he never told us what happened there. Not even my father knows the full story. After they came to the states, it was as if they took a vow of silence. Not just my grandparents, but my great aunts as well. My God." I sighed, "What had they suffered?"

Sobbing again, I could not get the image of my grandfather being tormented as a young Jew in Poland out of my mind. Finally, I looked up at Ariel and asked, "How in the world did a message as pure as the one the woman from Galilee shared, get so corrupted? She talked about a Man of love and immeasurable compassion, and one thousand years later, His followers are marching across Europe killing Jews as part of their devotion to Him. Help me understand!"

Ariel answered, "Indeed, these were *religious* people—but incredibly corrupted in their understanding of what true devotion to God really was. Yes, they were religious, but they were not practicing what is written in the Bible. Religion, apart from a true relationship with God, kills. Unsubmitted men will manipulate it for their own ends, be it lust for money or power."

"But didn't they read the Bible?" I asked.

"In time, David. All will be explained in time."

"In the story of the family in Spain, the Jews were being told, 'Convert or leave!' The Church there seemed more like the KGB or present-day Iran."

"You are correct, David. Those who converted were watched constantly by the Church to make sure they did not return to Judaism. *Conversos* accused of maintaining ties to or secretly practicing Judaism were cruelly punished."

I was struggling to process this.

"The Church of the Middle Ages had certainly ceased to look anything like what the Holy Spirit had birthed on that warm summer day on Shavuot, 30 CE, when the Jewish man, Simon Peter, preached so powerfully on the Temple steps, birthing a powerful revival. Instead, Rome had become a combination of greed, power, and politics dressed in the robes of religion. The good news had not merely been robbed of its

Jewish roots, but of its purity and power, its message of salvation and reconciliation to God."

Yes, I had read about Peter, the Christian evangelist, during my search for truth. But it hadn't dawned on me at the time that he was *Jewish*. But, of course he was! It all took place here in Israel.

"I am sure that you also noticed that the Jews in the first story had no qualms about believing that Yeshua was the Messiah. Not only was Chaya Jewish, but she met Him on His way to heal the daughter of one of the leaders in the local synagogue. Those first-century Jews were able to evaluate Yeshua without bias. However, two thousand years later, after the worst kind of anti-Semitism coming forth from those who claimed to represent Him, it is nearly impossible for a Jewish person to look at Yeshua without prejudice."

"We are taught, if not directly then indirectly, that one of the very definitions of being Jewish is that we don't believe in Jesus," I emphasized.

"When I was in elementary school, we had a discussion at the bus stop involving several Jewish children and Christian children. We were seeking to define the differences between our religions. After a lengthy exchange of views—our bus was always late—the 'Council of Cutshaw Avenue' concluded that the primary difference was that they believed in a man named Jesus and we did not. End of subject."

"Listen to the testimony of this rabbi." A man wearing a yarmulke appeared on the massive screen and began to speak.

Growing up in an orthodox Jewish household, I held great antipathy toward Jesus. The very name reminded me of the suffering laid upon Jewish communities for two thousand years: persecutions, forced conversions, expulsions, inquisitions, false accusations, degradations, economic exile, taxation, pogroms, stereotyping, ghettoization, and systematic extermination. All this incomprehensible violence and cruelty against us, against our friends and families, committed in the name of a Jew!

In my neighborhood, we did not even mention his name.[1]

"This rabbi, along with countless other Jews, could not help but factor in the Church's wide-ranging record of ungodly behavior when considering Yeshua. But what if Jewish people were able to appraise both the person and the message of Yeshua without any knowledge of either how the rabbis have viewed Him or how the Church has misrepresented Him?" Ariel pondered. "What if they could read the New Covenant without this bias?"

"I don't know that it could ever happen."

"Perhaps not, but you are with me, David, to receive an honest, accurate picture of this Man and His followers. No, it will not erase what you have learned from history, but it will give you the knowledge and capacity to discern history so that you will be able to differentiate Yeshua from religious fanatics who caused great damage to the Jewish people in His name."

Note

1. Shmuley Boteach, *Kosher Jesus* (Jerusalem: Gefen Publishing House, 2012), ix.

Chapter Seven

WHO KILLED JESUS?

Ariel continued, "While the Holocaust, unlike the Crusades and the Inquisitions, was not explicitly religious, the Church had set the stage. I am sure you have read the old axiom about Jews being called *Christ Killers*. The Nazis and others throughout the centuries have long enjoyed the employment of this claim as a satanic pretext for blood libels, pogroms, and Holocaust-scale genocide. In short, it is the excuse for nearly every perverted form of persecution that anti-Semitism has ever staged. And the enemy utilized all of this to further alienate Jews from their Jewish Messiah.

"Yes, *Christ Killer* has become a common moniker for Jews during these past 1,900 years. Under this theme, Jewish blood has flowed down the streets of not only Jerusalem, but numerous other cities as well."

"It never made any sense to me," I shared, "how an entire race of people over thousands of years of existence could be responsible for the killing of one man."

"Well David, who do you think *really* killed Yeshua?"

"I could make a case for the Romans, as Jews were forbidden from enforcing a death penalty. But I do know that it was Jewish people who handed Him over to the Romans."

Ariel helped, "Actually, David, it was primarily the Jewish *leaders*, not the people, who had a problem with Yeshua. I want you to read this."

As the words came out of his mouth, they appeared written in fire. Two passages of Scripture were before me, with some commentary in between. They were suspended in air and close enough for me to touch. I was in awe. "Go ahead, read!" I did.

> *Now when the chief priests and Pharisees heard His parables, they perceived that He was speaking of them. But when they sought to lay hands on [Yeshua], they feared the multitudes [of Jews]...* (Matthew 21:45-46 NKJV).

"In secret they found Him praying with His disciples at night, and only then did they dare arrest Him. In the morning, the day they planned to execute Him, the residents of Jerusalem were stunned to see this beloved Rabbi condemned. Read this next one."

Again, I read as I was asked.

*And a great multitude of the people followed Him...
who also mourned and lamented Him* (Luke
23:27 NKJV).

"Yeshua was taken to the home of Pilate. He was the
Roman governor over the province of Judea. Read on."

Again, emblazoned in fire I saw the Scriptures, but this
time certain words were highlighted:

*Then the detachment of soldiers with its commander
and the **Jewish officials** arrested Jesus...* (John
18:12).

*Then the **Jewish leaders** took Jesus from Caiaphas
to the palace of the Roman governor...* (John 18:28).

"While in the Greek," Ariel shared, "it merely says 'they'
in verse twenty-eight, it is understood that the 'they' in this
verse is referring to the Jewish officials in verse twelve."

"Ariel, I was told that the entire city of Jerusalem was
shouting for Him to be crucified. That would be more than
just a few leaders."

"Nowhere in the New Testament does it claim that the
entire city was calling for His death, but a crowd of people,
out of about a half a million who were in the city at the time...
and even this crowd had been worked up by the religious
leaders. But you are not the first to wrongly assume this. As
you will see on our journey, Yeshua was loved by the Jewish
masses and they came from all over the region to hear Him
teach. I want you to read a message that a Messianic Jew sent
to a Christian author on Facebook."

"*Facebook?* An angel who's into Facebook?"

61

"Well, I don't have my own account, but yes David, we kind of know about *everything*. Read!" Immediately, a Facebook page containing a message appeared on the screen.

> Dear Martin,
>
> My name is Avi Marks. I came across your website and I found your article, "Jesus and the Jews" very interesting; it was certainly well researched.
>
> May I just offer one critique that will help your Jewish readers? You used the phrase "the Jews" over fifty times. Sometimes it is just part of the phrase "king of *the Jews*." But more often than not, you are referring to the group of men who brought Yeshua to Pilate. John 18:12 makes it clear that it was not "the Jews" who brought Yeshua to Pilate, but "Jewish officials," "officers of the Jews," or the "Temple guards," just to quote a few modern translations.
>
> The problem with the way you use the term "the Jews," is that it makes it appear as if you are saying *all of the Jews*. There are a few times when you correctly say Jewish religious leaders, but for the most part you simply say, "the Jews."
>
> It is true that in the Greek, John at certain times simply writes the phrase "the Jews" (John 18:14; 19:7,12), but there can be no doubt that he is referring to the Jewish leadership. In fact, some modern English translations, such as the New International Version, actually translate those passages using the phrase "the Jewish leaders" as opposed to "the

Jews" even though they know that is not what the Greek says. How can they be so bold?

I'll explain. Take a look at John 18:14: *"Now it was Caiaphas who advised the Jews that it was expedient that one man should die for the people"* (NKJV).

In this passage it states clearly that Caiaphas was speaking to "the Jews." However, if we turn back a few pages we can see exactly to whom Caiaphas was speaking:

> *Then the **chief priests and the Pharisees called a meeting of the Sanhedrin**.... Then one of them, named Caiaphas, who was high priest that year, spoke up, "You know nothing at all! You do not realize that it is better for you that one man die for the people than that the whole nation perish"* (John 11:47,49-50).

So "the Jews" of John 18 and 19 are Jewish leaders, not the Jewish population. It would have been strange for those who flocked to hear Him teach—many of whom were healed—to suddenly call for His execution. Scripture makes it clear that a very large number of Jews followed Yeshua, even some high-profile leaders like Nicodemus.

> *When He had come into Jerusalem, all the city was moved, saying, "Who is this?" So the multitudes said, "This is Jesus, the prophet from Nazareth...* (Matthew 21:10-11 NKJV).

> *Many of the people believed in Him, and said,*
> *"When the Christ comes, will He do more*
> *signs than these which this Man has done?"*
> (John 7:31 NKJV).

> *Nevertheless, even among the* [Jewish] *rulers*
> *many believed in Him..."* (John 12:42 NKJV).

John records it was the leaders who shouted for Him to be crucified. "As soon as the chief priests and their officials saw him, they shouted, 'Crucify! Crucify!'" (John 19:6).

In the other accounts, where it mentions the crowd joining in, it seems clear they were manipulated by the leaders. As Matthew writes, "But the chief priests and the elders *persuaded the crowd* to ask for Barabbas and to have Jesus executed" (Matt. 27:20). We are not told the means by which they persuaded the crowd, but bribery would have been the common resource of the time. (They had paid witnesses to turn in false evidence at the trial the day before.) Clearly this persuaded crowd did not represent the people of Israel, as there were approximately 100,000 Jews living in Jerusalem, and because it was Passover, there could have been upward of another 500,000 visitors in Jerusalem at that time. Do you really think there were 600,000 Jews at Pilate's Jerusalem palace?

This may appear to you as nitpicking, but on the contrary, it is extremely important, because so many Jews have been falsely blamed for the death of Yeshua, even killed as part of this accusation of being *Christ-killers*. It is important therefore to make clear that it was primarily the Jewish leaders who were jealous of Yeshua who went to Pilate. The multitudes loved Him.

Thanks for your time.

Blessings,

Avi Marks

"This is crazy, Ariel. The entire Jewish nation has been blamed for the actions of a small group of jealous, politically oriented leaders and a manipulated crowd."

"I know, it is twisted and sad, but you should know not all the leaders were jealous of Him. Let the words of one of the passages that you just read, John 12:42, sink in." Again the words appeared in fire as Ariel read them:

Yet at the same time many even among the [Jewish] *leaders believed in him. But because of the Pharisees they would not openly acknowledge their faith for fear they would be put out of the synagogue* (John 12:42).

"These Jewish leaders believed, but were afraid. *Nicodemus*, to whom Avi made reference, was a Jewish leader, a member of the Sanhedrin, in fact. He was initially scared to be caught even speaking with Yeshua and so met with Him in secret, but eventually he became one of His most ardent followers."

Another passage in fire appeared.

Now there was a Pharisee, a man named Nico-demus who was a member of the Jewish ruling council. He came to Jesus at night and said, "Rabbi, we know that you are a teacher who has come from God. For no one could perform the signs you are doing if God were not with him (John 3:1-2).

"David, it is entirely false to claim, firstly, that all Israel rejected Yeshua, as you will see in the coming lessons; and secondly, that the Jews, or even the Romans for that matter, were responsible for killing Yeshua.

"Let me put this dreadful argument to rest—*I know who killed Yeshua.*"

"Who?" I asked, wondering what he would say. Wars have been fought over this question and now an angel sent from Heaven itself was about to tell me. *Unreal!* I thought.

"*You* did! *You* killed Him, David!"

Chapter Eight

"Me? A Killer?"

"What!?" I was incredulous. What was this angel talking about? "I am only twenty-eight years old. How could I have possibly killed Jesus?"

"Your sin nailed those spikes into His hands and feet," Ariel said with a holy passion, which prior to this he had not expressed. "It was your selfishness and rebellion that placed Yeshua on that Cross. Yes, David, you are the guilty one!

"But not just you, David, the whole world lies guilty before Him. It was the sin of the world—yours and that of everyone who came before you or will come after. If the world is looking for Christ's killer, it needs only to look in the mirror.

"Do you really think, David, that anyone could have killed the Divine Messiah without God's permission? Many times they tried to kill Him, but they could not, not until Yeshua allowed them to. Yeshua said it Himself. Go ahead and read, David."

The words of fire that were still there reformed into another passage and I read them aloud:

> *No one takes my life from me. I give my life of my own free will. I have the authority to give my life, and I have the authority to take my life back again...* (John 10:18 GW).

"This is in the New Testament?" I asked, astonished. He nodded. "How many Jews have been mistreated, even killed in the name of this blood libel, when all along the truth that He chose to die was plainly written in their Bible?" *I could feel myself getting angry again.*

"The Church erased the Jewishness of Yeshua and then blamed the entire Jewish nation for His death. This is why people, like you David, need to stop listening to what others tell them and do their own research. Notice that I am not teaching you anything that is not backed up by the historical account of Scripture...*and I have direct access to the Truth Himself.* When humankind has been given the divine revelation contained in the Bible, why would he then look to a human source to tell him whether or not Yeshua is the Messiah?

"Do you know how many times I have seen Jewish people, just like yourself, enter a season where the Father sends the Holy Spirit to draw them, to woo them, to attract them to Yeshua? They don't know why, but they are suddenly curious; they want to know. Seemingly out of nowhere, there is suddenly a deep concern over their soul. Is there a Heaven?

Is there a hell? Where will I spend eternity? This is how the Father brings new sheep into the fold. Yeshua Himself said when He walked the earth that 'No one can come to Me unless the Father who sent Mc draws them....' It is recorded in John 6:44.

"You know what most Jewish people do when they go through that season? Watch..."

The lights dimmed as the movie screen came back to life. I was stunned to see *me* there in the video! I was walking into Rabbi Goodman's office. Oh, I remember it well. I went there to confide in him—to tell him what I was going through, spiritually. When I spoke to him about my desire to find God, he was initially happy. Even when I told him I had researched different religions from the Far East, he remained pleasant, nodding benignly. But the minute I shared with him that I was intrigued by the story of Jesus, he became agitated, even angry.

"How could you, David? Your grandfather would roll over in his grave if he could hear you talking such nonsense. Don't you know what those people have done to us in His name? *And now you want to join them!*" He was getting angrier.

"I didn't say I wanted to join them, just that the Man Jesus and His purpose intrigue me," I countered. I felt humiliated and shamed.

He warned me in the strongest terms to end my spiritual journey if that was where it was leading me. "It will tear your family apart," he warned. As I left his office, I felt like a traitor for even considering Yeshua. At this point, the movie ended.

"Now, David, God has had mercy on you. Because of His plan for you I was sent, but you know as well as I, had I not pulled you out of that Starbucks you might never have considered Yeshua again." The word *never* hit me like a sword in my *kishkas*.[1]

I felt so ashamed that I had let Rabbi Goodman's intimidation keep me from seeking truth. "I am a writer, a journalist; I am supposed to look for the truth no matter where it takes me; and here, in the most important issue of my life, I caved in."

"David," he softly said, "I have watched that same scene played out thousands of times in the past twenty years alone. Jewish people who are wrestling privately with the issue of Yeshua go to their rabbi instead of the Bible, and get shamed out of continuing their search. While it breaks my heart, please understand that Rabbi Goodman meant no harm. He cares for you and your family. He was simply seeking to protect you. But, yes, he *was* wrong. Religious leaders have always sought to control the beliefs of their constituents. Before the advent of the printing press, the poor souls were completely dependent upon their leaders to tell them what the Bible said.

"There are some, though, who have thought for themselves. Today they are called Messianic Jews."

"I have heard of them. There is a large group right here in Philly...oh yeah...I am not in Philly, am I?"

Ariel laughed, "It's time for you, David Lebowitz, to rediscover the real Yeshua, the true Man, as He lived and died and rose from the grave, in this city—as a Jew. And then, you will offer *that* Yeshua, not a distorted facsimile of Him, to the Jewish people. The Lord has a task for you, but first we will expose this multifaceted, murderous identity theft that has caused so much pain. Are you ready?" he asked. Before I could reply, Ariel, my new friend, had grabbed me by the hand and we were flying again.

Note

1. Yiddish for "guts" or "soul."

Chapter Nine

CLASS IS IN SESSION

When we landed, we were in what I can only explain as a *high-tech, heavenly classroom*. Everything in the classroom was ancient and yet completely modern. For sure, it was the coolest room I had ever been in! There was a desk for me to sit at; it was made of Jerusalem stone. But the desktop was a tablet—I mean the desktop was a tablet as in Moses and the Ten Commandments-type tablet. But inside the stone tablet was an iPad-like interface. My tablet had a tablet!

The room was dimly lit in a yellowish-orange glow, as if lit by a torch or lantern. In fact, it wasn't unlike the synagogue in Jerusalem, except for the fact that we appeared to be suspended in space and moving though at a very slow pace!

There were no walls or ceilings, and I could see the stars and moon above me. There was a floor beneath us made of ancient, off-white marble, which made up the size of the classroom. I had the feeling that the marble was about a yard thick beneath me, but I couldn't really see.

In the front of the room was another tablet, only it was massive, about twelve feet by four feet and it had the face of a computer monitor—a very modern, large, and cool computer monitor. There was one file on the screen. It read, "DL 1.0."—my initials. *This was crazy. It had to be a dream.*

I had an insatiable desire to learn, which I can't adequately explain in human terms—especially since it was the first time I'd ever experienced it. All I can say is that I felt like my brain had been programmed to optimum absorption and I couldn't wait to start learning.

"This will be our homeroom, David. You will spend a good deal of your time here learning, but don't get too comfortable, as we will go on several journeys.

"Let me lay some ground rules. I will be showing you passages from books, encyclopedias, even websites, and of course, God's Word, so that you can prepare for your assignment. Everything I show you here will be saved on your tablet on your desktop in the classroom. You see, David, I am not going to tell you what to believe, but I am going to help you build your case, primarily based on the Scriptures, but backed up by history. I will show you the evidence, but in the end, you must decide.

"I am doing this for two reasons. First, you will use this information in fulfilling your destiny. Second, I don't want you to trust a word I say theologically, if it is not backed up by Scripture. This is how many people are deceived. Paul wrote to the Galatians that even if an angel comes to you, if it is another gospel, reject it! (See Galatians 1:8.) Mohammad and Joseph Smith are just two of the more famous individuals who were deceived by false angels. Everything must line up with God's Word.

"And, we will study history. For all you know, I could just be making up stories, but if I supply you with the documents to back it up, not only will it be credible but, back to point one, you will be better equipped to convince others."

Convince others—what was he talking about?

"Let's begin," Ariel was now dressed in professorial garb of cap and gown like in a prep school. "We will start with names. I do not deny that names are important," he began to lecture. "They are. But at the risk of contradicting myself, I would also warn you not to get too hung up on names. The Father is not looking to catch us on technicalities. Sadly, there are those who obsess over names and miss the essence of the person of Yeshua."

Ariel tapped the center of the file that read DL 1.0 and suddenly the computer within the ancient tablet came to life. Several men appeared. The first one said, "Unless you read the Bible in the King James English, you are not reading the Bible!"

The second one said, "If you are not baptized according to our church's constitution, you are not saved and you're on your way to hell."

The third and last one proclaimed, "If you don't pronounce His sacred name correctly, you will be damned."

Ariel was laughing. "Silly religious people—this is not the God of the New Covenant, who 'is not willing that any of these little ones should perish.'"

As he said this, I heard a sound, not unlike the one my cell phone emits when I get a new text message. Right on cue "No. 1: Matthew 18:14" appeared on the right side of my personal tablet.

"There is no angel at the gates of Heaven ready to say, 'Sally, we really would like to let you in. Your heart was pure, you loved people and sacrificed for the kingdom, *but* we got you on a technicality. You got a name wrong and so you're disqualified. Sorry about that!'"

Oh, so my angel is a comedian.

"No!" He continued, becoming serious again. "God is looking for every opportunity to save. People who get caught up in names, genealogies, traditions, or rituals and overemphasize their importance have a *religious spirit,* and that is not a good thing, David—it blinds them to the love of God, and sometimes to God Himself. Paul warns Timothy about those who promote controversy rather than God's love."

The text message sound and another verse appeared on my desktop, again with a number beside it: "They have an unhealthy interest in controversies and quarrels about words that result in envy, strife, malicious talk, evil suspicions" (1 Tim. 6:4).

My tablet desktop was taking notes for me. *I could've used one of these in college,* I thought.

"Sadly, there's always the danger of getting so hung up on the minutiae that we miss the very purpose of Yeshua's coming, which was, 'to seek and save those who are lost.'" A third passage appeared—Luke 19:10 NLT.

"Having said that, if we are going to understand the New Covenant in context, we are going to have to review a few names, as these name changes and translations influence how we perceive both the culture and message of certain New Covenant characters. These name revisions have resulted in both Jewish and Gentile readers completely missing the fact that these people were Jews, with Jewish names. Revisions that have tragically obscured the Jewishness of the New Covenant, communicating incorrectly to Jews that the New Covenant is not Jewish."

"D'ling," announced the appearance of Jeremiah 31:31 on my tablet:

> *"The days are coming," declares the Lord, "when I will make a new covenant with the people of Israel and with the people of Judah."*

"David, while English versions of the New Covenant refer to Yeshua by His Greek name, *Iesous*, which when translated into English becomes *Jesus*, His parents never called Him by either of those names. Joseph, His stepfather, was given very specific instructions as to what His name was to be and why." My tablet promptly displayed Matthew 1:20-21:

> *An angel of the Lord appeared to him in a dream and said, "Joseph son of David, do not be afraid to take [Miriam] home as your wife, because what is conceived in her is from the Holy Spirit. She will give birth to a son, and you are to give him the name [Yeshua], because he will save his people from their sins"* (Matthew 1:20-21).

Ariel continued his lecture, "The name *Yeshua*, in Hebrew, actually has meaning. Just about every Hebrew name has a meaning or comes from a similar root with a meaning, and the angel was very specific about the name that the Son of God, the Messiah, should have: His name was to be *Yeshua*. Pronounced slightly differently, putting the emphasis on the last syllable instead of the middle, *ye-shu-à* means *salvation*. In essence the angel told Joseph, *'His name shall be "salvation" because he will "yoshia" (verb form, save) His people from their sins.'* It is impossible to pick up on this prophetic word play in the Greek or English versions.

"And that, of course, was the mission of the Messiah, *to bring salvation to His people and to be a light to the nations.* Indeed, Simeon, the aged prophet who had been told he would not die until he saw the Messiah, prophesied as much."

Then I saw an old man on the larger tablet begin to pray, tears streaming down his face, as he held a baby in his arms. This had to be the Simeon of whom he spoke.

> *Sovereign Lord, as you have promised, you may now dismiss your servant in peace. For my eyes have seen your salvation, which you have prepared in the sight of all nations: a light for revelation to the gentiles, and the glory of your people Israel* (Luke 2:29-32).

"His name was *salvation* because He would bring *salvation*."

"The name *Yeshua* was also a shortened form of the name *Joshua*, which in Hebrew is pronounced *Yehoshua*. In later books of the Hebrew Bible we find the Hebrew name *Yeshua* and it is translated as *Joshua*. (See Zechariah 3.) Joshua means 'the Lord is salvation,' or 'the Lord saves.' Tell me David, what sounds more Jewish to you, the name *Jesus* or *Joshua*?"

"Well Joshua, of course," I answered.

"In the Greek, both Joshua and Jesus are exactly the same: *Iesous*. But when referring to the Messiah, they translated His name as *Jesus*. When Joshua is mentioned in the New Covenant, they do not translate His name as Jesus, even though in the Greek it is the same, but use the Hebrew transliteration—Joshua—leaving us to think they are two different names. As a result, we lose the Jewish character of Jesus's name. While Joshua is seen as Jewish, the Jewish Messiah has been portrayed throughout history as being something other than Jewish."

"So Joshua and Jesus are the same name?"

"Don't be so amazed, David. There is more.

"All your life you were probably told that the mother of Yeshua was a woman named Mary. In fact, millions of people actually call her Maria. Why is this significant? It's important because these names make the mother of Yeshua sound English as in *Mary* or Italian as in *Maria*, when of course she was neither. She was not the lead role in *West Side Story* or Jimmy Stewart's wife in *It's a Wonderful Life*."

"How do you know about movies, Ariel?"

"Stay focused, David."

"I always viewed Mary as a Roman Catholic teenager," I offered.

Ariel chuckled and said, "That would have been difficult, as she was born in Israel several hundred years before there ever was such a thing as the Roman Catholic Church."

"Well, what about this *mother of God* business? They worship her and pray to her in some cultures."

On the larger tablet appeared a woman, a precious woman. She began to talk to me. "David, this breaks God's heart and mine as well. I am just a woman, a very blessed one, but nothing more. The Father never intended that people would pray to me or worship me. While it is difficult to be sad when you are constantly in the presence of the Almighty, what people have made of me disturbs me greatly. And what is worse is that the very people who claim to adore me have oppressed my people. They pray that I will intercede for them, and at the same time they persecute and kill my descendants. I am an Israelite, and my name, by the way, is Miriam, *a Jewish name*—the same name as the sister of Moses."

"So why is your name printed as Mary in the New Testament, but the sister of Moses is *Miriam*?" I asked her.

"Oh, I'll let Ariel explain that. He's the expert. I shared what I needed to share. Bless you David," and the board was empty again.

"The answer is simple," said my eager angelic teacher, "and it is not as sinister as you may think, although it still confuses the identity of Yeshua's earthly mother. The New Covenant was written in Greek so her name had already been *Hellenized*—that is, conformed to Greek culture. Even in the original text, they wrote the Greek equivalent of her name rather than her actual name. And the English translation of the Greek form of Miriam is *Mary* or *Maria*. Whereas when the Hebrew Scriptures were translated into English, there was no Greek influence. Thus, Moses's sister remained Miriam.

"One more thing, David—while Miriam was correct in saying that she was not divine, I don't want to sell her short. She was chosen for a reason. She was a humble, loving, God-fearing servant of the Lord. She has taken her place next to

Sarah, Rebecca, and Rachel in the kingdom. She is a very special woman and should have been an example to young Jewish girls throughout the centuries, but like Yeshua, her identity was greatly altered, even hijacked."

"This is really new to me," I responded. "But, I have a question."

"Shoot," said Ariel.

"Okay, this *John the Baptist* character; if you are saying that the New Covenant is Jewish, who is this guy? I mean, he is a *Baptist*, for crying out loud. How could there be anything Jewish about him?"

The massive tablet came to life again and a fellow wearing some sort of caveman outfit appeared. He was laughing at me.

"Tell me something, Dave," he chuckled. "If I mentioned the name *Ezekiel* would you think Jewish or Christian?"

"Ezekiel was a Jewish prophet, so Jewish, of course."

"How about *Jeremiah, Daniel, Isaiah*, or *Haggai*?" the man asked.

"Well they were all prophets from the Hebrew Scriptures, so once again, Jewish."

"Right, Dave."

I didn't appreciate this caveman character calling me *Dave*. My name is David.

"Okay, I'll call you David," he laughed again.

"But how—I didn't say anything."

"No, but you thought it and I'm a prophet, which is not a mind reader, of course, but if the Lord allows it, I sometimes see things, and I saw that you didn't want to be called *Dave*, okay David?"

"O...kay," I uttered uneasily.

"David, getting back on point," the prophet continued, "if I mention the name *John the Baptist*, what do you think of?"

"Well Christian, right?"

Then he yelled out, "*Booooom! Gotcha!*"

I was startled. This guy was a hoot.

"My name is John, actually Yochanan in Hebrew, and I was *not* a Baptist. And here is another shocking revelation for you: *There were no Baptists at that time—although they seem like fine folk*," he said jokingly in a southern accent. In his normal voice, he continued, "The truth is, David, I was a Jewish prophet and I died, actually I had my head handed to me on a silver platter—literally!—years before anyone had ever used the word *Christian*.

"In the manner of Ezekiel, Jeremiah, and Isaiah," he became serious, "I was honored to be the last and greatest of the Jewish prophets who proclaimed the coming of the Messiah in fulfillment of prophecy."

A sound signaled new activity and Isaiah 40:3-5 appeared on my tablet.

"Sadly, I died prior to the New Covenant, but it was important for me to get out of the way," he added with feigned annoyance, "although it would have been nicer to simply die in my sleep—and keep my head!

"David, the only difference between me and my predecessors was that my ministry was recorded in the New Covenant. They called me *the Baptizer* because when my *100 percent Jewish* followers would repent, I would immerse them in water, symbolizing spiritual cleansing. Funnily enough, the practice did not begin with the New Covenant or as a Christian tradition; immersion in water had been common practice in Judaism as a form of ritual cleansing for centuries before I implemented it in my ministry.

"In fact, outside the Temple in Jerusalem were nearly fifty *mikvot*—immersion tanks—for Jews wishing to make a sacrifice at the Temple. The ministry of immersion with which the Lord entrusted me preceded and prepared the people for Yeshua's coming. It was not something new to the people of Israel. They understood its significance. The fact that thousands of Jews 'from Jerusalem and all Judea and the whole region of the Jordan,' went out to be immersed by me attests to this fact."

Matthew 3:5 appeared on my tablet. "The fact that people now associate me and my signature with a denomination that began only five hundred years ago and that they don't see me as a Jew is truly sad, because it takes the Jewish context away from the Gospel narrative. God called me, a Jewish man, to call the Jewish people to prepare themselves for the Jewish Messiah."

The screen on the larger tablet went blank.

"I liked him, Ariel."

"I should let you know that the people you are meeting do not look as they appear to you. It was decided that for the purposes of our investigation each of these figures would appear to you as they would have appeared on earth during their lifetime," Ariel explained.

"Good to know. I was hoping people didn't dress like cavemen in Heaven!"

We had a good laugh. Ariel and I were becoming friends.

Chapter Ten

PETER THE POPE?

"Have you heard of Peter?" Ariel asked.

"Eh, yeah, he was one of the first followers of Je—I mean Yeshua, right? Wasn't he the first pope?"

I thought Ariel was smiling because I began to refer to Jesus by His Hebrew name, but he was chuckling at my assertion that Peter was the first pope.

"Okay, D'vid" he used the Hebrew pronunciation of my name, "there are two issues with Peter—his *name*, and his *function*. Let's start with his name. First of all, it wasn't Peter. The word *Peter*, or *Petros* in Greek, simply means *rock*. Peter's real name was Simon, or Shimon in Hebrew. However, on the occasion he received the revelation and declared that Yeshua was 'the Messiah, the Son of the living God...'" Matthew 16:16

appeared at the top of all the previous passages that had been sent me on my tablet. "Yeshua announced that henceforth..."

"*Henceforth*? Who talks like that?" A strong, well-muscled individual with a big bushy beard now occupied the screen. He was confident and clearly had a sense of humor. "Angel, just let me tell my story. David," he turned to me, "I really think you would rather hear it from me. I don't use any of those three-dollar words like Professor Ariel over there."

"Oh yes, you are a brilliant communicator. The problem is, you don't know when *not* to talk!" Ariel then mimicked, "Lord, it is good for us to be here. If you wish, I will put up three shelters—one for You, one for Moses and one for Elijah," reminding the man of his ill-timed words on the Mount of Transfiguration (see Matt. 17:4).

"Yeah, yeah, yeah, you can remind us of that or you could tell him about my sermon on Shavuot...or before the Sanhedrin when they told us to stop preaching the Gospel! I remember it like it was yesterday, 'Rulers and elders of the people! If we are being called to account today for an act of kindness shown to a man who was lame and are being asked how he was healed, then know this, you and all the people of Israel: It is by the name of Yeshua, the Messiah, that this man stands before you healed...salvation is found in no one else, for there is no other name under Heaven given to mankind by which we must be saved' (see Acts 4:8-12).

"In truth it wasn't that difficult. Even though He had gone, He was still with us. We couldn't see Him, but man, we could feel Him. Yeshua's presence was almost tangible. The miracle of healing we'd just witnessed—a paraplegic jumping up and down, praising God—and the fact that we were now doing what we'd watched Him do so many times, empowered us. We felt as bold as lions—not afraid of any man!"

"Okay, Fisherman, you got it right more than you got it wrong so I guess we could let you share for a bit." They both laughed.

"Where were we...oh yes, when I had the revelation that Yeshua was the Messiah, the Son of God, He gave me a new name—*Kefa*!

"*Kefa* means "rock" in Aramaic, the commonly used language of the time. It's very close to Hebrew. However, when the New Testament was written in Greek, in most places they did not transliterate my name. Do you know what that means?"

"Sure, that's when you take a word from another language and spell it with the letters of your own language to enable you to pronounce it, even though you may not know what it means," I offered.

"Exactly," said Simon Peter. "My name was rarely transliterated to Greek which would be *Cephas*. In most places, they translated it to *Petros*—the Greek word for "rock," which in English is *Peter*. Yeshua, however, never called me *Petros*, but only *Kefa* or *Shimon Kefa*."

Scripture references appeared on my tablet: John 1:42; First Corinthians 1:12; 3:22; 9:5; 15:5; Galatians 2:9,11,14.

Ariel interrupted, "The problem with using the name *Peter* is the same as with *John* or *Mary*. They are fine names; they just take away from the Jewishness of the narrative. Your average Jewish person has no idea that the man Christians call Peter is actually Jewish.

"This brings us to the second issue, regarding his *function*. When Yeshua told Shimon that He would build His Church on this *rock*, He was referring, not to Peter the man, but to the revelation Shimon had been given, that He, Yeshua, was 'the Messiah, the Son of the living God.' This revelation would be foundational to receiving salvation—and to the nature of the *Kehilah*."

"*Kehi*-what?"

"*Kehilah*. It's a Hebrew word that means community. I want you to use it when referring to the community of followers of Yeshua. Many people use the word *church*. Church comes from the Greek word *kyriakon*, which is not in the New Covenant. The word that is translated church is *ekklesia*, which means, 'called out ones' or 'those called to assemble' and comes from the Hebrew word *kahal*, which means, "audience" or "assembly." *Kehila* also comes from *kahal* and means 'community.' *Ekklesia* is a great word, because those who follow Yeshua are called out from the rest of the world and are grafted into the Commonwealth of Faith, the Father's household. No matter what you think of the word *church*, a word is only as powerful as its meaning to its hearer, and most people hearing the word church today think of buildings, not people.

"For instance, if someone said to you 'David, look at that church,' what would you be looking at?"

"A building, I guess?"

"That's correct; at least in the way the word is most commonly used today. But if someone said, 'I belong to a *community*,' you would think of people, not a building, right?"

"Makes sense."

"Okay, back on topic—the Roman Catholics misinterpreted Yeshua's words to mean that He was bestowing special authority on Kefa. From this distorted interpretation, a doctrine later emerged that taught that *Kefa* or *Peter* himself was *the rock* upon which Yeshua would build his Church.

"Centuries later, this misinterpretation extended to the Roman Catholics' claiming that Shimon Kefa was the first pope."

Shimon began to laugh, "I don't know what's crazier, that there was a pope in the first century or that he was *Jewish*! Can you imagine me, Shimon, wearing that outfit the popes wear, or letting people kiss my ring? And how about that hat?" We were all laughing now.

"It's called a mitre, Shimon, and we need to move on now," Ariel gently chided the fisherman. Still laughing, Shimon disappeared from the screen.

"Roman Catholics maintain," Ariel continued, "that Peter was the primary leader of the early believing community, and that he eventually moved to Rome and became the first bishop of Rome. Through apostolic succession, every bishop of Rome after Peter would be the head of Christianity."

"Apostolic *what*?" I asked.

"Apostolic *succession*. It is the belief in the uninterrupted transmission of spiritual authority from the apostles through successive popes and bishops. Roman Catholics mistakenly maintain that Peter passed his authority down to the next pope and so on and so forth. Many denominations believe in the idea that there has been unbroken transfer of apostolic authority from the apostles to the present, but the Roman Catholic Church additionally believes the Pope's authority on matters of faith and morals is divinely inspired and sanctioned."

"So you are saying that Peter's authority was passed down to the second pope, and then he gave it to the next one, all the way down to today's pope...and that they are therefore incapable of making mistakes?"

"No, *I* am not saying that, *Roman Catholics* say that. This bishop of Rome, or the Pope, was regarded as authoritative when it came to issues of doctrine and morality for the Church. It was maintained that, without its leaders, the Church would move into deception. Later on, they would declare that the Pope's dogmatic teachings on faith and morality were infallible.[1]

"It is true that the Father raises up leaders to guide His people..." The text message sound prompted me to look down:

> So [Messiah] *himself gave the apostles, the prophets, the evangelists, the pastors and teachers, to equip his people for works of service, so that the body of* [Messiah] *may be built up until we all reach unity in the faith and in the knowledge of the Son of God and become mature, attaining to the whole measure of the fullness of* [Messiah]. *Then we will no longer be infants, tossed back and forth by the waves, and blown here and there by every wind of teaching and by the cunning and craftiness of people in their deceitful scheming* (Ephesians 4:11-14).

"...But they are always subject to the authority of His Word. God never expects us to blindly follow a man, especially one who claims he is incapable of making mistakes. As the passage says, leaders are given to His followers to bring them to maturity, so they can think for themselves—not to keep them enslaved to one man's dogma."

I remembered again how I allowed my rabbi to make me feel guilty over my interest in Yeshua. I know he meant well, but he was basically asking me to trust him and not seek truth on my own.

"Either it is ridiculous," Shimon was back, "or Yeshua changes His mind a lot, because Roman Catholic doctrine has changed quite a bit over the centuries, with a number of popes contradicting the edicts of other popes. There are even examples of violence and intrigue between popes and would-be popes.

"Believe it or not, David, many of the popes were far more *political* than *pious*. The first bishop to adopt the title of pope was a guy named Saint Damasus. He was accused of adultery and led murderous raids against his enemies, killing over one hundred and sixty people! He was anything but a genuine believer.

"Another pope, Symmachus, around the year 500 CE conducted what can only be described as a holy war against his enemies. As the two groups fought in the streets, killing scores of men, one of the pope's ardent followers declared that the pope was 'judge in the place of the Most High, pure from all sin, and exempt from all punishment.' All who fell fighting in his cause, he declared, enrolled on the register of heavens.'"[2] The quote appeared on my tablet.

I responded, "Throw in a few virgins, and this sounds eerily similar to the radical Islam of today."

"You're so right," exclaimed Shimon. "Religion is religion no matter what name you give it. It is easier to get people to fight for your cause if they are willing to die, and it is a lot easier to get them to be willing to die if you promise them paradise on the other side—plus something extra to appeal to their carnal lusts, like seventy-two virgins. For a destitute, uneducated Arab teenager who doesn't see much of a future ahead of him, this promise is very attractive."

"It was the same with a lot of the Crusaders you showed me, right Ariel? Many of them were poor peasants who suddenly found purpose and identity through fighting for the Church, even if it was misguided."

"You are catching on quickly, David," responded the angel.

"Another pope, Stephen VI," Ariel was not to be distracted, "had the body of a previous pope exhumed and dressed in his Episcopal robes so he could stand trial. He was found guilty. This mock trial also declared all of Pope Formosus's ordinations to be invalid. Apparently he was not as infallible as once thought."

"This is crazy!" I maintained. "How can this be true? I see the Pope on TV and he hardly seems capable of such things."

"Fortunately the Catholic Church has changed—for the better, I might add—over the years. And to be clear David, there have always been true followers of Yeshua in the Roman Catholic Church. Many of the bishops throughout the centuries truly loved Yeshua and sought to serve Him. In fact, there were several popes who genuinely sought to serve the Lord, but this sad history, one that most Roman Catholics don't even know, did indeed take place. And David, it is important that I prepare you for your future task ahead and that requires taking an honest look at history."

"Okay guys, I've already heard this, so I'm going to leave now. David, it was an honor to meet you." And he was gone.

Future task ahead? An honor to meet me? I wasn't even sure if I believed any of this was happening—and here was Peter of the Bible telling me that he was honored to meet me!

Ariel interrupted my reflections, "Now concerning Peter or Kefa and the belief that he was the first pope..." suddenly on my tablet opposite the Scriptures, under the heading, "Notes" were listed four points.

"Read those out loud please," Ariel requested.

"Number 1. While it is clear from the early chapters of Acts that Peter—that is, Kefa—was the greater among equals, the senior leader among the apostles, it is also clear that Kefa gave himself to traveling ministry (Acts 8, Acts 10) and turned over this responsibility to James..."

"Actually, his name was Jacob," Ariel interrupted me, "but we will come to that later." I continued reading.

"...The brother of Yeshua, as he was clearly the one in charge in later chapters, both in Acts 15 where Shimon Kefa testified and in Acts 21 when Paul visited Jerusalem. Furthermore, in Galatians 2, Paul writes 'When certain men came from James to Antioch where Peter was,' proving both that Peter was sent out to Antioch from Jerusalem and that Jerusalem was the headquarters.

"Who is Paul? You mentioned him earlier," I asked.

"Soon, David, just keep reading."

"Number 2. Peter clearly wasn't infallible as we see in that same Galatians 2 passage. Here Paul rebukes Peter publicly for his hypocrisy in refusing to eat with Gentiles when certain men came from Jerusalem, though he freely ate with them before these men arrived. The tradition of the elders, which would become the oral law, forbade Jews to eat with

Gentiles. This was not a biblical issue, but one of tradition—a bad tradition.

"Number 3. There is no record in the New Covenant, or in history, of Peter ever being the bishop of Rome.

"Number 4. And last, while there is evidence Peter visited Rome, we never see him portrayed as the Bishop of Rome. And even if he had possessed this position, where is it written in the New Covenant that the Bishop of Rome would hold the seat of authority over Church doctrine—ever? Let alone, forever? If such an idea were even biblical, Jerusalem, not Rome, would have been the obvious choice, as the Acts 15 Council, the first doctrinal conference of elders and apostles, was held in Jerusalem. And of course we know that Yeshua does not return to Rome to set up His millennial kingdom, but to Jerusalem." (See Zechariah 14:1-4.)

"I know that some of these things are probably a bit confusing to you, David—'Millennial Kingdom,' 'Jerusalem Council,' etc. I realize that much of this is new, but just stay with me and it will all be clear in the end. The main point I want you to see here is that God never intended for there to be any central authority on earth that controlled the faith and doctrine of every believer. He alone holds all authority, and it is to Him and to His Word that men must come. People can, and should, read His Word for themselves."

Notes

1. This doctrine was adopted by the Roman Catholic Church in the First Vatican Council of 1869-1870.

2. G.W. Foote and J.M. Wheeler, *Crimes of Christianity* (London: Progressive Publishing Co., 1887), 123.

Chapter Eleven

NICE JEWISH BOYS: SAUL, JACOB, AND JUDAH

"David, you asked about Paul. He is the central author of the New Covenant—at least of the letters to the congregations—and his name was actually Saul of Tarsus. He was both Jewish and a Roman citizen, not to mention a rabbi of the Pharisees. He studied under Gamaliel, one of the most respected rabbinical scholars of his day. He was so zealous for God and convinced that Jewish people who believed in Yeshua were deceived that he sought to arrest Jewish believers and even approved the stoning to death of Stephen, a leader among the first Jewish believers."

Acts 7:58–8:1 appeared and I made a mental note to look it up afterward. Right now, I was hanging on the angel's every word. "However, on his way to Damascus to arrest Messianic Jews—Jews who believe in Yeshua—he was knocked to the ground and blinded by a great light. I remember that day! We angels weren't too crazy about this guy. I mean, he was throwing Jewish believers in jail and even having some killed! But the Father said, 'This man is my chosen instrument to proclaim my name to the Gentiles and their kings and to the people of Israel. I will show him how much he must suffer for my name' (Acts 9:15-16).

"At the time, I quietly thought, *He deserves to suffer all right*, but couldn't quite see how this guy would ever be preaching to the Gentiles. But, as always, Father knows best.

"Yeshua had a little chat with Saul on the Damascus road and convinced him that he was on the wrong side of the issue. After this dramatic encounter, he became a believer and actually began to share the good news of Yeshua with Jewish people. In fact, he immediately went into the synagogues and began preaching."

"Wait a minute! Are you telling me that the primary writer of the New Covenant was a Jewish rabbi,[1] and that after persecuting believers, he became one himself and actually went into Jewish synagogues preaching about Yeshua?"

"You're starting to get it, David," he said with a big grin.

"Well, why don't Jewish people know this?" I demanded.

"That is why you are here David—to answer that exact question! But not quite yet." He continued telling Paul's story. "Many years later, as he traveled throughout the known world seeking to help both Jews and Gentiles discover a dynamic, personal relationship with the King of the universe, the Bible refers to the fact that he had two names." On my screen appeared: "Then Saul, who was also called Paul..." (Acts 13:9).

"Sadly, for centuries Christians have taught that Saul changed his name to Paul after he became a believer. In other words, he had to get rid of his Jewish name and take on a Christian one."

"But Paul," I jumped in, "is a Latin name and was popular in Rome long before Christianity. If anything, it would be connected to Rome, which was pagan and polytheistic."

"Right David, and let's not forget. At the time that Paul was preaching, Rome was anything but a friend to the believing community. In fact, Rome became the primary persecutor of the body of believers, the Kehilah, for the first three hundred years."

Just then a gray-haired English vicar appeared on the screen. He was addressing his congregation:

> "The Roman emperor Nero had the believers tied to poles in the garden, covered with tar and set on fire to illuminate his garden parties. And then he would take other believers and sew them into the skins of wild beasts and set dogs on them to tear them to bits to entertain his guests. And I have stood in that garden and wondered how many believers died a horrible death for his barbecue parties."[2]

"It is highly unlikely that Saul changed his name to reflect this barbaric culture. What's more, if Saul truly changed his name from a Jewish one to a Roman one, then why did he wait so many years after coming to faith to do so?"

"Then why does it say he was also called Paul?" I asked.

"Let me ask you this," Ariel replied. "Do you have a Hebrew name?"

"Of course. Anyone who grew up in a Jewish home outside of Israel knows that it is common for Jewish people to have two names, one that relates to the culture in which they live, and a Hebrew name. Mine is Chaim."

"Ah, Chaim, a great name. It means *life*," Ariel commented, then continued. "When Saul was traveling in non-Jewish areas, he used his Roman name, Paul, and when in Israel or amongst Jews, he used his Hebrew name, Shaul. Saul is its Anglicized equivalent. Notice the passage doesn't say, 'Saul, who changed his name to Paul,' but rather, 'Saul, who was also called Paul'—as, *in addition to*, not *instead of*.

"Some of the smartest Bible teachers in the world miss this simple fact. This pastor you are about to see (a man standing behind a pulpit appeared on the flat screen but in pause mode) is an excellent Bible teacher and he loves Israel. He and his church have given sacrificially to Jewish believers. But listen to him in a recent message."

Ariel played me just one sentence. I couldn't tell you the context of his sermon but I simply heard him say: "Saul was on the road to Damascus. That is what his name was *then*."

"Here is another one. This man's messages are listened to by millions every week online." Another man appeared. "Paul, his *original* name was Saul..."

"This fine preacher, well-versed in the Scriptures, simply assumes that Shaul changed his name. If people so bright can miss this simple point," Ariel noted, "how easy has it been for the enemy to rob Saul, the second most prominent figure in the New Covenant, of his Jewish identity and thus confuse the nature of the New Covenant for Jewish people?" Ariel noted. "Earlier I mentioned James to you," Ariel said, switching subjects.

"You said his name was actually Jacob."

"Good, you're paying attention!" Paying attention was an understatement. I felt like I had a supernatural ability to absorb information. "Well I want you to meet Jacob, the physical half-brother of Yeshua."

The screen of the massive tablet lit up again and a handsome man in his thirties said to me, "Yeah, they sure did a job on my name. 'James,' for Heaven's sake! No one ever called me James, not growing up, not ever! If they had, you might assume I was the butler or the chauffeur!" James was laughing. "But nope, I'm Jewish and grew up in Galilee."

"You...grew up...with...*Yeshua*?" I tentatively asked, making sure I used the name that Jacob would have known Him by. How surreal it was to be talking to someone who actually grew up in the same house as Jesus!

"Yeah, and it wasn't easy. Try growing up in the shadow of the *Ma-Sye-Ya*!" he raised his voice for emphasis, but was smiling. "In all seriousness, it wasn't easy. It took me a long time before I believed—imagine your half-brother telling you that His other genealogical half is God! But after His resurrection, there was no denying that indeed, my brother was the Messiah. After I became a believer, others quickly looked to me for leadership, simply because I grew up with the Messiah. I resisted this at first—I had doubted Him for so many years. However, to my surprise that is exactly what He called me to do—to lead this new group of believing Jews in Jerusalem, along with Kefa and the other apostles, in following the Risen Messiah—my brother.

"I'll let Ariel take it from here. I just wanted to meet you." And he was gone.

Like Shimon Kefa, Jacob wanted to meet *me*? Who was I?

"David," Ariel continued his lesson, "in just about every other translation of the New Covenant—German, Hungarian, French, etc.—the word *James* is properly translated as *Jacob* or *Yakov*."[3]

"So why is it *James* in English?" I asked.

"Many have speculated that since King James authorized the English translation of the Bible, translators did this to honor him, but actually the names Jacob and James had been synonymous for some time. The Latin name *Iacomus* (James) was very close to the Latin for Jacob, *Iacobus*, and it appears that it was just a linguistic corruption or confusion. Nevertheless, it has been a costly one.

"The problem, once again, with this mistranslation of Jacob is that it lessens the perception of the New Covenant as a Jewish document. If a Jewish person, like you David, opened up the New Testament to the book of James, you would wrongly conclude that this James had no connection with Judaism or Israel. However, if the book, which was addressed to the twelve tribes of Israel scattered abroad, was properly entitled Jacob, your reaction would be just the opposite—you would instantly recognize that he is Jewish. It would convey and reinforce to you the Jewish context[4] of the New Covenant. I want you to meet Jacob's brother."

"*Yeshua*!" I exclaimed, terrified.

"No, He had other brothers. David, meet Judas."

A shiver went down my spine. I was afraid to speak.

"Relax, David, I am not *that* Judas."

"Who are you then?"

"I am Jacob's brother, like Ariel just said, which makes me, yes, the half-brother of Yeshua. I know that Judas Iscariot, who betrayed Yeshua, is more famous, or I should say 'infamous,' than I, but I did write one of the books of the New Covenant, albeit a very short one, creatively titled after yours truly. The problem with the other Judas, in addition to the fact that he was a thief and a traitor, is that his name has become synonymous with 'traitor' in modern vernacular and in many dictionaries."

On my tablet I saw: "Judas: *someone who betrays under the guise of friendship*, Webster's Dictionary."[5]

"But no one, thankfully, ever actually called me by that name. My name is Yehuda, or Judah in English, the same name as the fourth son of Jacob, of the tribes of Israel."

Ariel took over, "As in the case of the name of Yeshua, had they skipped the Greek and simply transliterated from Hebrew to English, my friend here and his book would be known today by the name *Judah*.

"*Judah*, or *Yehuda*, means 'praise,' from the same root word we get *Judaism*, the name of the Jewish religion. When ancient Israel was separated into two kingdoms, the southern kingdom was named Judah. Modern-day Israel still refers to the southern region of the territories that she recovered in the Six Day War as Yehudah."

"Ariel, it seems that there has been a concerted effort to make the followers of Yeshua look very *non*-Jewish. Not only has Yeshua's identity been altered, but also His first followers; even His brothers appear to have undergone a *Gentile make-over*. I didn't know any of this! And I know that my Jewish friends and family don't know it either."

"David, we are just beginning. This is only the tip of the iceberg. Here, take my hand."

We were flying again.

Notes

1. Formal rabbinic ordination did not begin until about forty years later, but *rabbi* was the term of honor given to a respected Jewish teacher in Paul's day.

2. Adapted from a message given by David Pawson at Brisbane Gateway Centre in April, 1998 entitled, *What Hope for the Millennium?*

3. *James* appears in Spanish Bible as "Santiago"; it is derived from *san* (meaning *saint*) and *Diego*, which comes from Jacob—but changed a lot along the way. Nevertheless, it has no connection to the English name James.

4. It is also interesting to note that in Jacob (James) 2:2 when it refers to the meeting place of believers, the Greek word that is translated *meeting* in the NIV and *assembly* in the KJV is *synagogē*, from which we derive the English word *synagogue*. This was not a blatant attempt to change the meaning of the word because synagogue, while associated today with Jewish houses of worship, does mean assembly. However,

if the New Covenant translators simply used the obvious English equivalent, synagogue, it would have sent a different message to Jewish people.

5. Webster's Online Dictionary, s.v., "Judas," accessed August 10, 2012, http://www.websters-online-dictionary.org/definitions/judas.

Chapter Twelve

THE LAST SUPPER
OR SEDER?

Once again, we were going back in time. Above me were only stars, while below I could see time periods passing me by. They looked like scrolling movie film and I could make out the names—the Industrial Revolution, the Revolutionary War, Napoleon, and Louis the Sixteenth. And as we again drew closer to the ground, I knew we were back in Jerusalem. It was evening, and the city was bathed in soft golden light, as torches illuminated almost every courtyard.

We hovered over one home in midair and I realized we were defying gravity. We were able to see right through the roof. It was as if it were transparent. A group of people were sitting around a long table.

"What do you see?" asked Ariel.

"A dinner party."

"Look more closely," he exhorted.

"I see a Kiddush Cup, for blessing the wine, and that looks like matzah. Is it Passover? Are they having a Seder meal, the meal we eat on the first night of Passover?"

"Indeed they are, but this is no ordinary Passover Seder. Look a little closer, at the people."

"Wait a minute. I recognize Peter, I mean Kefa. Is this what I think it is?"

"Yes, it is the Last Supper; and tomorrow Yeshua will die."

"Are you telling me that the Last Supper was a Passover Seder meal?"

"What else would you expect Jews to be doing on Passover in Jerusalem—celebrating *Festivus*?"

I have an angel who knows Seinfeld jokes, I thought.

"Look on your screen." I did and saw:

Then came the day of Unleavened Bread on which the Passover lamb had to be sacrificed. [Yeshua] *sent Peter and John, saying, "Go and make preparations for us to eat the Passover."*

"Where do you want us to prepare for it?" they asked.

He replied, "As you enter the city, a man carrying a jar of water will meet you. Follow him to the house that he enters, and say to the owner of the house, 'The Teacher asks: Where is the guest room, where I may eat the Passover with my disciples?' He will

show you a large room upstairs, all furnished.
Make preparations there."

They left and found things just as [Yeshua] *had*
told them. So they prepared the Passover.

When the hour came, [Yeshua] *and his apostles*
reclined at the table. And he said to them, "I have
eagerly desired to eat this Passover with you before
I suffer" (Luke 22:7-15)

"When you see Leonardo da Vinci's painting of the Last Supper, you don't think *Jewish*. If I remember correctly, he has bread on the table! It's Passover, for goodness sake; Jews don't eat bread on Passover!"

"What do you expect from an Italian painter in 1495? The Church had already drifted so far from its Jewish roots, no one would have even thought to bring it to the painter's attention. In Spain they were already killing Jewish converts who returned to Judaism. Why would Leonardo emphasize the Messiah's Jewishness? In fact, doing so could have put his own life in jeopardy."

"That makes sense," I agreed. "So Yeshua died on the first day of Passover?"

"Yes, but there is more." Ariel and I were flying again. This was a very short trip. We landed on a grassy knoll near some large rocks. I realized later that they were tombs.

"Where are we?" I asked.

"No, '*When are we?*' is the correct question. And I'll give you a hint—in Heaven we don't call this day *Easter Sunday* any more than we call the Passover you just saw *Good Friday*. Read this passage David."

This time it was a cloud that formed in the shape of letters. But it was in Hebrew. "Ariel, I can't read Hebrew. I mean, I can sound out the words but I have no idea what I am saying." Most Jewish boys in America learn how to read the Hebrew alphabet for their bar Mitzvahs, but rarely do we actually learn the language.

"Try," he said with a mischievous grin.

So I did, and I found I could both read and understand Hebrew! Amazing! The verse said: "He is to wave the sheaf before the Lord so it will be accepted on your behalf; the priest is to wave it on the day after the Sabbath" (Lev. 23:11).

"Ah...so? What does this mean to me, today?" I asked.

"David, this passage is from Leviticus 23. Adonai tells the Israelites to bring a Firstfruits offering before the Lord on the first Sunday after the first Saturday, or Sabbath, after Passover begins. On this day the priest would wave a sheaf before the Lord. It is called the Feast of Firstfruits. Shaul, remember him? He wrote this: 'but now [Messiah] is risen from the dead, *and* has become the firstfruits...'" (1 Cor. 15:20 NKJV).

This time it was in English and I was beginning to grasp the significance of what he was showing me. "Is this the day Yeshua rises from the dead? And if so," my thoughts were racing, "you are telling me that not only did He die on a Jewish feast day, but He also rose from the dead on a Jewish feast day?"

"*Bingo!* Such a good student you are," and he actually pinched my cheek in jest. "But David, this is not just any Jewish feast day! It is the Feast of *Firstfruits!* Yeshua rose from the dead, as Shaul said, as its fulfillment. He is the Firstfruits of God's harvest, and millions have followed Him. The same power that raised Him from the dead lives in them, giving them life everlasting. I imagine you would like to experience that, too?"

I could experience it, too? This was what I was looking for. Yes, I want that joy, that peace; I want that serenity I saw in Kefa, Jacob, and Judah. And they are Jews! I am not turning my back on my people. They *are* my people! This is what I have been searching for!

"Ariel, I'm ready. I want—*Ariel?* Where are you?" Finally, I was ready and my angel just disappeared. Unexpectedly there was a commotion behind me. I turned around and saw two women who looked absolutely terrified and a few Roman guards on the ground trembling with fear. Then I saw *why*. The massive covering stone had been removed from one of the tombs and two men in gleaming garments were standing beside them. No, they weren't men. They were like Ariel... wait...it *was* Ariel! At least, one of them was. As they began to speak, their words formed in little clouds in front of me. I read as I heard them say to the women:

> ...*Why do you look for the living among the dead?*
> *He is not here; he has risen! Remember how he told*
> *you, while he was still with you in Galilee: "The*
> *Son of Man must be delivered over to the hands of*
> *sinners, be crucified and on the third day be raised*
> *again"* (Luke 24:5-7).

When Ariel reappeared by my side, I said excitingly something akin to, "You were...you...ah."

"Yes, I was chosen to join Alexander in announcing that the King—the King of the Jews—had risen from the dead."

I was beginning to understand that I was with no *Private First Class* angel. This dude had some clout. And what did that say about the fact that he was sent to me? What did all this mean? I'm just a writer from Philadelphia.

"That was an amazing day, that was," he wasn't even talking to me. "There was rejoicing in Heaven on a scale none of us had ever seen before; not even when Moses parted the Red Sea."

"You were in on that, too?"

"No, but I watched it."

"My rabbi once told me that the Israelites passed through the *Reed* Sea, not the *Red* Sea and that the water was only a few feet high."

"Tell your rabbi that if he's right, then an even greater miracle happened on that first Passover!"

"What do you mean?"

"All of Pharaoh's army drowned in only two feet of water!"

We both laughed out loud as he took my hand again. Being somewhat analytical, I realized that I wasn't just laughing because he was funny, but because I was with an angel, 2,000 years in the past and I was happier than I had ever been in my whole life. Happy isn't even the right word. I was beyond happy. I was ecstatic! I felt a joy beyond my ability, even as a writer, to express. Later I would find the term "joy unspeakable" in the New Covenant—and that summed it up perfectly!

We were flying again but in daylight this time. When we landed, we were still in Jerusalem, but at the ancient Temple. We hovered above the courtyard and I noticed the city was packed.

"Why are all these people here?"

"Today is the day of Shavuot, one of the feast days on which Jewish pilgrims from all over the region come to Jerusalem to celebrate. It marks the ending of the forty-nine day counting of the Omer, from *Firstfruits*, the day Yeshua rose from the dead, to *Shavuot*, the Feast of Weeks. Sadly, most Christians know this feast day only as the Day of Pentecost, a Greek word meaning "fifty." Greek-speaking Jews would also have used this word, but the difference is that they knew it was a Jewish or biblical feast day. Most Gentile Christians know it only as the day that the Holy Spirit fell upon and empowered the believers, birthing the Kehilah."

"Can you unwrap that for me further? The Holy Spirit fell? What does that mean and why is this Jewish festival important to Christians?" I asked.

"Ten days ago, forty days after His resurrection, Yeshua told His followers, about 120 of them, to wait in Jerusalem for the Holy Spirit to empower them. He told them that once empowered, they would take this message, the message of forgiveness of sin and redemption through His sacrifice, not only to Jerusalem and Judea, but also to Samaria and even to the ends of the earth. Look."

The cloud returned and I read, "But you will receive power when the Holy Spirit comes on you; and you will be my witnesses in Jerusalem, and in all Judea and Samaria, and to the ends of the earth" (Acts 1:8).

I reached out and waved my hand through the cloud. The letters scattered, but then returned to form sentences again. *Unreal,* I thought. Suddenly there was a loud sound. It seemed to come from the sky, like a windstorm, and could be heard from afar.

"Look down David," Ariel instructed.

When I did, I could see a large group, I assumed the 120, gathered in an enclosure that was part of a colonnade.[1] I saw what looked like flames of fire resting over the heads of each of the believers there, who were now praising God loudly in different languages. They seemed intoxicated with joy. "There is Shimon Kefa," I blurted out, as he made his way into the Temple courtyard, followed by the others.

"Keep watching," Ariel was smiling.

The noise like a mighty wind, the flames of fire and the spectacle of Galileans speaking in foreign languages had quickly drawn a crowd of curious Jewish bystanders, which was growing larger by the minute.

"Oh, so this is what he was talking about when he proudly referred to his sermon on Shavuot. He is going to speak now, right?"

Ariel nodded, as Kefa stood up, "Men of Israel!" he declared. Kefa was right. This was an amazing moment. I had never heard anyone speak like this—certainly not in my synagogue. With passion, authority, and insight into the Scriptures, he proclaimed that Yeshua was Israel's Messiah. His hearers were deeply moved. All these Jews, many of whom had come from other nations for Shavuot, appeared to be stunned by the rough fisherman's dynamic delivery. Even the other believers were looking at Kefa with new respect and amazement, as if to say, "Is this the same Shimon Kefa that we know?"

"This is the same Kefa who, only fifty-three days ago, denied that he even knew Yeshua!" Ariel said.

"What!?"

"I am afraid so. It was just after Yeshua was arrested. A young servant girl accused him of being a disciple of Yeshua. He swore up and down that he wasn't. Kefa was a gaffe machine! One minute he declares that Yeshua is the Messiah, then the next, he is telling Yeshua that he won't let Him go to the Cross. And then he denies even knowing Him—not just once, but *three* times!

"Afterward, he was so ashamed. But Yeshua, after His resurrection, immediately reassured Him of His love and forgiveness and affirmed that he would have a significant role to play in His kingdom—no, not as the Pope," he smiled, "but as one of the greatest communicators of Yeshua's message there has ever been!

"I'll let you in on a secret. The Father doesn't always choose the ones that others would. He took the youngest son of Jesse, David, and made him king over Israel. He chose Joseph, the hated brother of the sons of Jacob, who was sold as a slave, and made him the second most powerful leader in the world—just in time to save from starvation the very same brothers who had wanted to kill him. And here, He takes an impulsive, uneducated, burly fisherman and gives him a gift like no one has ever seen before. The Father is far more interested in a person's heart than in their talents. And Shimon has a great heart. Take a look."

After hearing his message, the men cried out to Kefa and the other apostles, "Brothers, what shall we do?"

Kefa didn't hesitate, "Repent and be immersed in water, every one of you, in the name of Yeshua, the Messiah, for the forgiveness of your sins."

The crowd began to weep, as people openly confessed their sins. It was like someone took a collective blindfold off of these Jews and they saw clearly that they were in need of forgiveness. This was nothing like Yom Kippur in my synagogue. Every year we all dress up and come to the congregation to pray. We fast for twenty-four hours—many without even water. We spend the morning reading prayers that someone else wrote, confessing our sins—but never in tears! Never like this. I wouldn't say it is a joke, but neither is it taken seriously. At least now I could see that. It wasn't unlike the state of these people *before* the Holy Spirit fell upon them. They had come to Jerusalem out of religious obedience, but hadn't actually expected to have an encounter with God.

The apostles organized the crowd and used what appeared to be a system of baths (*mikvot*), to immerse these people in water. Thousands went into the water and came out on the other side. As they did, they were glowing. They entered with tears of anguish and guilt at the realization of their sin, but emerged with tears of joy. Many were actually dancing with each other as they came out. In fact, it reminded me of the story of Miriam and the Israelites dancing on the other side, having passed through the Red Sea unharmed. The city was in an uproar. And while I could see that these people's lives were being radically changed, I couldn't understand why a Jew would be baptized.

"What is happening? Why are these Jews being baptized?" I asked Ariel.

"Remember what John told you earlier—immersion in water *began* with the Jews. These *mikvot* or immersion pools have been in existence for centuries. It was the practice of all those coming up to Jerusalem to present an offering at the

Temple to first be made ritually clean by passing through these waters.

"The problem is that most Jewish people, when they hear the Greek word *baptism*, tend to think of the Middle Ages, when so-called Christians forced Jewish people to be baptized in water, symbolizing their conversion from Judaism to Catholicism, just like Christophe in our story earlier. To the Jewish mind, baptism is not equated with coming to faith in the Jewish Messiah or seen as a sign of dying to the old nature and rising to new life, but rather it is equated with persecution, expulsion, and even physical death.

"But as you have just seen for yourself it was not like that in the beginning. Thousands of Jews, plus their wives and children, joyfully and *willingly* entered into the waters of immersion, seeing it as something entirely Jewish, which it is."

Written before me appeared an archeological reference in cloud-like letters as before:

> A series of public ritual bathing installations were found on the south side of the Temple Mount. Because of the stringent laws regarding purity before entering holy places, demand for *mikvot* was high and many have been discovered from first century Jerusalem.[2]

"The difference is that immersion in water during the Temple period was something that needed to be repeated over and over again, each time one would come to the Temple to make a sacrifice. In the New Covenant, it is something we do only once, when we come to faith—as these have done today—and it symbolizes dying to our old life and entrance into a new life with God. Just look at their radiant faces—it's so obvious, they've undergone a life-changing experience."

A passage appeared.

> *Or do you not know that as many of us as were baptized into* [Messiah Yeshua] *were baptized into His death? Therefore we were buried with Him through baptism into death, that just as* [Messiah] *was raised from the dead by the glory of the Father, even so we also should walk in newness of life* (Romans 6:3-4 NKJV).

"Unbelievable!" I was beside myself. This journey was endlessly amazing. "Ariel, do you realize that Yeshua *died* on a Jewish feast day—on Passover? And that He *rose from the dead* on the Jewish feast of Bikurim, Firstfruits. And then, He *poured out His Spirit* for the first time on His followers on the Jewish feast of Shavuot. It's almost as if God was trying to impress upon the world that this thing is *Jewish!* Am I right?"

"You're preachin' to the choir," Ariel was beaming. "However, within a few decades, the number of non-Jews who would join the *Kehilah*, the community of believers, would far outnumber the Jews, and the Father was laying a blueprint that would ensure people never forgot that salvation began with the Jews."

"But they did forget," I offered. "The Christianity in most of those stories, the movies you showed me, bears no resemblance to anything that I've seen here today. The Church changed so much over the centuries that Yeshua was no longer even recognizable as the Jewish Messiah of Israel. And it was not just His name that was changed, but

His very nature. They made it seem like Yeshua was against the Jews!"

"And," Ariel interrupted, "they conveniently forgot that He'd said that He had been sent *to the lost sheep of Israel,* and that, not only were all His followers Jewish—He was Jewish Himself! Furthermore, according Jeremiah, the New Covenant would be made with the house of Judah and the house of Israel!" (See Jeremiah 31:31.)

"Even baptism," I jumped back in, "they managed to turn into something altogether foreign to Jews. Nor was it ever emphasized, if the Church was even aware of it, that all these powerful milestones of Christianity, like His death and resurrection, took place on Jewish holidays.

"And another thing—why do Christians worship on Sunday when the Sabbath is clearly from Friday evening to Saturday evening? If this all started with Jews, why would they change the Sabbath?"

"You wanna go there? Okay then, I guess we can take a look at it." The angel *stretched*, feigning exhaustion. "But we will need to return to the classroom first. Hold on to me."

Instantly, we were flying again. *I would never get tired of this!*

Notes

1. While it has been a longstanding view that the 120 were at the Upper Room, many modern-day scholars, including Daniel Juster and Richard Longenecker, as well as the NIV Study Bible authors, not to mention the 19th-century scholar Adam Clarke (Clarke's Commentary on the Bible) and many others believe the disciples were in the Temple,

probably in an enclosed area as part of Solomon's Portico or porch.

"When, moreover, we bear in mind the fact (which appears both from the Scriptures and from other contemporary records) that the Temple, with its vast corridors or 'porches', was the regular gathering place of all the various parties and sects of Jews, however antagonistic the one to the other, it will be easy to realize that the Temple is just the place—both because of its hallowed associations, and also because of its many convenient meeting places—where the disciples would naturally congregate. Edersheim says that the vast Temple area was capable of containing a concourse of 210,000 people; and he mentions also that the colonnades in Solomon's Porch formed many gathering places for the various sects, schools and congregations of the people. In commenting on John 7 this trustworthy authority says that the gathering places in Solomon's Porch 'had benches in them; and from the liberty of speaking and teaching in Israel, Jesus might here address the people in the very face of his enemies.' It was, moreover, and this is an important item of evidence, in Solomon's Porch that the concourse of Jews gathered which Peter addressed in Acts 3 (see verse 11). Hence there can be little doubt that one of the assembling places to which Edersheim refers was the 'house' where the disciples were 'sitting' when the Holy Spirit came upon them." (Philip Mauro, The Hope of Israel: What Is It?, 1922, accessed August 10, 2012, http://www.preteristarchive.com/books/1922_mauro_hope-israel.html#CHAPTER_X.)

Let us also consider that this was on the morning of Shavuot, one of the most significant days of the Jewish year. It was the custom of the disciples to worship and pray in the

Temple courtyard daily—how much more on Shavuot? Luke records: "While he was blessing them, he left them and was taken up into heaven. Then they worshiped him and returned to Jerusalem with great joy. And they stayed continually at the Temple, praising God" (Luke 24:51-53). This passage refers specifically to the ten days immediately after the ascension leading to Shavuot.

Furthermore, the Upper Room, at least the place where it is believed to have been, is a good twenty-minute walk from the Temple Mount and the immersion pools. The throng of Jewish pilgrims who witnessed the outpouring would have been at the Temple on Shavuot, as that is why they had journeyed to Israel. At the very least, if it was a home, it had to be adjacent to the temple.

2. "Southern Temple Mount," Excavations (BiblePlaces.com), Mikveh, accessed November 17, 2012, http://www.bibleplaces.com/southerntm.htm.

Chapter Thirteen

CELEBRATE THE SABBATH AND FORFEIT YOUR SALVATION!

Back in the classroom, the lesson began...

"In the year 364 CE, at the Council of Laodicea, the Church formally declared Sunday as the Lord's Day, the day of worship and rest, effectively changing the Sabbath from Saturday to Sunday—at least in their minds. The pervading sentiment of the Council is given expression in this quote from Canon XXIX:

> Christians shall not Judaize and be idle on Satur-
> day, they shall work on that day; but the Lord's Day
> they shall especially honor; and being Christians,

shall, if possible, do no work on that day. If, however, they are found Judaizing, *they shall be shut out from Christ.*[1]

"These believers were not merely discouraged from celebrating the Jewish Sabbath, they were *commanded not* to do so. If they *did*, they would be 'anathema from Christ,' as another English translation of the same quote says. That means they would be, in the eyes of the Church—but not the Father's, mind you—cut off from the Church and the Messiah—in short *excommunicated.*"

"How could they do that if it is not expressly written in the New Covenant? Where did they get the authority to do such things?" I asked.

"That goes back to the Kefa debacle. Remember when we talked about how the Roman Catholic Church misinterpreted Yeshua's comment to Kefa?"

"Yes," I said, marveling that my capacity to absorb information here was at least ten times what it had been when I was in university. "Yeshua was saying that the rock He would build His Kehila on was *the revelation that He is the Messiah, the Son of the living God*. Roman Catholics believe that Kefa *himself* was the rock, and that is why they assume he was the first pope."

Ariel added, "From there they somehow concluded that Kefa, 'the first pope,' had special authority when it came to issues of doctrine, and so every pope after him had this same authority. This really gave them *carte blanche* when it came to dogma. They could basically make up whatever served their purposes, whether it was in the Bible or not, and then declare that it was binding—not because God had said it, but because He had given them the authority to do so. In fact, later they would claim that not only did the Pope have permission to establish doctrine, but that he could not err in doing so—he was infallible. He was preserved by God from error. It is taught that this was an expression of God's love to protect the Church from deception, which is in fact why we have His Word. In truth, this was invented so that the Church could control the people and the Pope's authority over doctrine was drilled into them. For example, in *The Convert's Catechism for Catholic Doctrine*, the question is asked, 'By what authority did the Church substitute Sunday for Saturday?' The answer: 'The Church substituted Sunday for Saturday by the plenitude of that divine power which Jesus Christ bestowed upon her.'[2]

"The Scriptures are the highest authority for the body of believers. Yet they base this change not on the authority of Scripture, but upon their own misguided reasoning that the Father had given them authority *beyond* Scripture," Ariel concluded. "Over the centuries the Church has abused its authority, using it to manipulate those dependent upon its leadership for guidance."

"That's horrible. How does God react to people who take their own ideas and turn them into hard and fast doctrine? They don't even give scriptural support for their ruling because they claim, 'The Church has authority.'"

"Well David, He gets downright *langry!*"

"*Langry?*"

"Yeah, I made it up, it means that first He laughs at how utterly ridiculous it is for mere men, His creation, to pretend that they speak *for* Him without first speaking *to* Him—and then He gets angry.

"In Psalm 2, when speaking about the nations' attitude toward Yeshua and Jerusalem, He also gets *langry*." My tablet signaled new activity, as Psalm 2:1-6 materialized.

> *Why are the nations so angry? Why do they waste their time with futile plans? The kings of the earth prepare for battle; the rulers plot together against the Lord and against His anointed one. "Let us break their chains," they cry, "and free ourselves from slavery to God." But the one who rules in heaven* **laughs***. The Lord scoffs at them.* **Then in anger he rebukes them, terrifying them with his fierce fury.** *For the Lord declares, "I have placed my chosen king on the throne in Jerusalem, on my holy mountain"* (NLT).

"I always picture the United Nations when I read that passage. All those little people wielding too much authority, pretending that they can out-vote God. You humans are something else, you know—heads of nations parading around with their entourages, feeling very important. From our vantage point, they look like ants—ants who talk too much!

"You see David, Yeshua's idea of leadership is so totally different from man's."

The board flickered and, as on a movie screen, I saw Yeshua and His disciples. I was fascinated by what I witnessed. The meal was ending as Yeshua got up from the table. He took off His outer garment and wrapped a towel around Himself. *What was He doing?* I noticed that the faces of His disciples were equally mystified as He took a large washbowl and carefully filled it with water. Then placing it on the floor beside Him, He knelt down and started washing their feet.

What impressed me most was the manner in which He did it, showing all the tenderness and love with which a mother would wash her infant child. Don't get me wrong, the man I was watching was 100 percent masculine; His hands were strong and angular. *The hands of a carpenter,* I thought. Hadn't Chaya shared in her story earlier that He was a woodworker by trade?

Having carefully washed the feet of each one of them, Yeshua was resisted by Peter alone, who at first protested and then consented to the act of servanthood and affection. Yeshua then drew the towel from His waist and, exhibiting the same gentleness, dried their feet...at which point the image faded from view.

"Impressive, huh?" said the angel.

"Wow." I wiped a tear from my eye. "Such love and humility," I marveled. This short scene really touched me. "But why did Kefa object?" I asked.

"Kefa felt like many of us would—he felt it wasn't right for someone of Yeshua's standing to lower Himself and do the work of a servant, but that was exactly the point He wanted to make. To be a true leader you had to be willing to be a servant. He was setting an example.

"That is the model of New Testament leadership," Ariel shared, "but rarely does a man lead from love. Most aspire to leadership for reasons of selfish ambition; to boost their ego, to have control or to compensate for some lack in their own self-esteem. But Yeshua said that to be a leader you must be the servant of all, and He set the example, not only by washing the feet of His protégés, but by laying down His life for all humankind.

"Here is one of the most ancient creeds of the first believers."

Who, being in very nature God, did not consider equality with God something to be used to his own advantage; **rather, he made himself nothing by taking the very nature of a servant**, *being made in human likeness. And being found in appearance as a man, he humbled himself by becoming obedient to death—even death on a cross!* (Philippians 2:6-8)

"Good leadership will always be accompanied by a deep concern for the welfare of those under their authority. Because of His great love, He left Heaven—He left the Father's side—to come to earth.

"Furthermore, when human leaders make decisions without consulting God's Word, or that are contrary to God's will, they invariably end up doing more harm than good. They fail to see the big picture, and can only guess at how their actions or decisions might affect those who will come after them. It was the same with this Council. They thought changing the Sabbath was harmless back in 364 CE, but now, with the benefit of hindsight, we can clearly see how the edict not only provided the groundwork for future persecution of the Jews but sadly erected an insurmountable barrier to Jewish people even considering Yeshua."

A new passage appeared on my tablet: "But as he came closer to Jerusalem and saw the city ahead, he began to weep" (Luke 19:41 NLT).

"Luke records that Yeshua was weeping over Jerusalem because they hadn't recognized the day of their visitation. But," Ariel expanded, "His weeping was not for that generation only."

As the scene unfolded before me, I saw Yeshua gazing down upon Jerusalem as He made His way down the Mount of Olives. His soul was in anguish as He saw the suffering of His people down through the centuries; suffering which could have been averted had they only recognized and welcomed their Messiah

As He began to weep, it was as if I were seeing what He saw. And together we watched a series of scenes unfold, one after the other:

First, I saw the Romans destroy the city in 70 CE, the Temple being destroyed and the city burned. Thousands were massacred—men, women, and children.

Then I saw the Romans crush the Bar Kokhba revolt in 135 CE Those murdered were too numerous to count. For ten years, the Jews were not allowed to bury their dead. Jerusalem was renamed Aelia Capitolina, referencing false gods, and Judea was renamed Palestine, as the Emperor sought to disassociate it from the Jewish people. Jews were barred from Jerusalem. Then I saw a series of blood libels, where Jews were accused of kidnapping Christian children and using their blood in the making of matzah (a patently ludicrous accusation in light of the Jewish food laws which prohibited the eating of blood). Tragically, countless numbers of Jews—whole communities, were killed.

Next, I saw the Crusaders overtaking Jerusalem, butchering almost the entire city.

This was followed by Inquisitions—Jews being tortured, forced to convert, or expelled from their countries.

Next I saw a Ukrainian man, whose name I instinctively knew was Bohdan Khmelnytsky. This leader and instigator of hundreds of pogroms murdered tens of thousands of Jews in the most vicious and sadistic ways, most of whom had previously fled other nations where they were not welcome to come to Poland, a nation considered a safe haven for Jews until Khmelnytsky came on the scene.

"Stop!" I screamed. "I can't take anymore!"

"You made it further than most. Still, it's a drop in the bucket compared to the burden that Yeshua carries. He sees it all, past, present, and future. When He wept over Jerusalem, it wasn't merely for the Jews of that time. He was able to see the terrible persecutions that awaited them in the future, both in Israel and in the Diaspora...*and it broke His heart*."

The Messiah's image faded from view as I wiped beads of sweat from my brow. "I thought we were talking about Sunday worship. How did this get so intense?"

"Interesting you should say that, because those responsible for the seemingly innocuous act of changing the day of worship didn't realize either that it would lead all the way to murder and even genocide.

"Okay. Are you ready to continue now?"

"Can you promise to keep it light?"

Notes

1. John Nevins Andrews, *History of the Sabbath and the First Day of the Week* (Washington, DC: Review & Herald Publishing Assoc., 1912), 409.

2. Rev. Peter Geiermann, *The Convert's Catechism of Catholic Doctrine* (St. Louis: Herder Book Co., 1946), 48.

Chapter Fourteen

"Theory" Trumps "Commandment"?

"Other well-meaning Christians have bought into different theories about why the Sabbath was changed or should be changed, but that's all they are, theories. None of them in any way abrogates Exodus 20."

> *Remember the Sabbath day by keeping it holy. Six days you shall labor and do all your work, but the seventh day is a Sabbath to the Lord your God. On it you shall not do any work, neither you, nor your son or daughter, nor your male or female servant, nor your animals, nor any foreigner residing in your towns. For in six days the Lord made the*

heavens and the earth, the sea, and all that is in them, but he rested on the seventh day. Therefore the Lord blessed the Sabbath day and made it holy (Exodus 20:8-11).

"It would seem to me," I offered, "that to change something so explicit—one of the Ten Commandments—you would need an equally explicit command."

"Exactly. There are of course those who hold the view that since we are now no longer under Law but under grace, that we no longer need to keep the Sabbath. If followed to its logical conclusion, this argument would remove any obligation to keep the other nine of the Ten Commandments as well—Heaven forbid that believers embrace adultery, thievery, and murder because they are 'no longer under the Law.'

"Another commonly held idea is that because the resurrection occurred on the first day of the week and is referred to as the Lord's Day, another error which we will cover in a few minutes, it now supersedes the Sabbath as the day of worship or celebration."

"But there is actually nothing in the new Testament that specifically says the Sabbath was changed to Sunday." I reiterated.

"Nothing! Now that doesn't mean that there are not a few passages that have been misinterpreted. For instance, Yeshua appeared to His disciples as they were gathered together on the Sunday on which He rose from the dead."

"But they weren't having a service, were they? They had just two days earlier witnessed their leader being executed. I imagine they spent most of their time together after that."

"Yes, you are right, David, but some say they were together on Sunday, when Yeshua appeared to them again a week later, according to John's Gospel."

The white screen hummed to life and a character I'd not yet met appeared.

"Hello David, my name is Toma, some call me *Doubting Thomas*, but that really isn't fair. It was just the one time and you have to admit, it had been a rough few days for all of us."

"Really? What about when you blurted out on the way to raise Lazarus from the dead, 'Let's go, too—and die with Yeshua'?" Ariel was laughing.

"That wasn't *doubt*, Angel; that was *courage*. I was willing to die. So I misunderstood the mission. But still, I was ready to pay the ultimate price. And concerning His first appearance, don't forget I hadn't seen Yeshua and the others had. I'd arrived late that first night He appeared to them, and missed seeing Him. So naturally I was pretty skeptical about it all. Who wouldn't be? It had been an extremely stressful time. I thought they were probably seeing things. You know, lack of sleep and all that. Anyway, I am here because I've got a message for my Jewish brother here. You ready, David?" Toma asked.

"Sure." I liked his personality.

"Okay. Even though I missed the first meeting, I made sure I was there for the second meeting—not that we knew when He would come back. I just made sure that I stayed close to home. And as it turned out, my brothers weren't so crazy after all."

A passage appeared on my tablet that read, "A week later his disciples were in the house again, and Thomas was with them. Though the doors were locked, Jesus came and stood among them and said, 'Peace be with you!'" (John 20:26).

"I nearly jumped out of my skin!" exclaimed Toma. "I was standing there talking when I felt a tap on my shoulder and turned around. And there He was, smiling the biggest smile. You could tell He was enjoying it.

"'Peace be with you,' He said. *Peace?* I nearly fainted."

Ariel interrupted him, "What day of the week was that?"

"If you knew Greek," Toma became more serious, "you would know that it doesn't actually say a week later, but *eight days* later! Now I know that some have argued that the counting included resurrection Sunday, but *I was there!*"

"Well?" I asked, "Which was it—Sunday or Monday?"

"Let me ask you something first," said Toma.

Oy, these people are always answering questions with questions, I thought.

"If you were going to refer to a week from now, would you say, 'in seven days' or 'in a week'?" asked Toma.

"'In a week,' of course," I answered.

"Right, so if someone chooses to say 'eight days,' they probably don't mean a week, because if they did, they would simply say 'a week,' not 'eight days.'

"But honestly, *who cares?*" Thomas shouted, throwing up his hands. "It doesn't matter. Of course we were there! We were there on Sunday and Monday and even on Tuesday—we were *living* in the Upper Room. We were not Judeans, but Galileans. Our homes were several days away—and we didn't have cars, trains, or buses back then. We were holed up in the Upper Room, wondering what in the world to do.

"In both accounts, if you noticed, the doors are locked. That was pretty uncommon in those days, if you were at home—and we had eleven men there. Why would eleven men hide behind locked doors? I'll tell you. *We were scared!* Even though the other brothers had had that one encounter with Yeshua a week, or 'eight days' earlier," he winked, "we had not seen Him since. And remember—they *did* kill Him. So yeah, we were still scared, pretty nervous, and shaken up."

Chapter Fifteen

SATURDAY NIGHT'S ALL RIGHT

"Furthermore," Toma continued, "the Kehilah had not yet come into being. The last thing on our minds was devising some new order or routine for meeting. We were so broken; we had no idea that we would even stay together as a group, much less meet every week. Kefa was still so ashamed that he had denied that he ever knew the Messiah. However, after Shavuot everything changed.

"We did begin to meet. Would you like to know on what day? Read these two passages."

I read.

> **Every day** they continued to meet together in the
> temple courts. They broke bread in their homes and
> ate together with glad and sincere hearts, praising

God and enjoying the favor of all the people. And the Lord added to their number daily those who were being saved (Acts 2:46-47).

"This next one is right after we were beaten because we refused to stop preaching in Yeshua's name!"

The apostles left the high council rejoicing that God had counted them worthy to suffer disgrace for the name of [Yeshua]. *And every day, in the Temple and from house to house, they continued to teach and preach this message: "[Yeshua] is the Messiah"* (Acts 5:41-42 NLT).

"Every day, David, *every day!* In the Temple and from house to house. It was an amazing time, looking back. We had miracles and signs and wonders and best of all, the presence of God. Yeshua was so close to us. It was simply the best time..." As Toma was reminiscing, he faded from the screen.

"David, remember the passage I shared with you in the beginning; it should be number three on your list."

"Yeah, I've got it here." I read it aloud. "'The days are coming' declares the Lord, 'when I will make a new covenant with the people of Israel and with the people of Judah'" (Jer. 31:31).

"With whom is He making the New Covenant?" asked the teacher.

"With Israel and Judah."

"You understand that at that time, when Jeremiah gave the prophecy, the people of Israel were divided into two kingdoms, Israel in the north and Judah in the south. So in essence, He is making this New Covenant with all of Israel, right?"

"Right," I agreed.

"Now tap twice on the passage," Ariel requested. When I did, the entire thirty-first chapter of Jeremiah opened up. "Read verse thirty-three please."

> *"For this is the covenant I will make with the house of Isra'el after those days," says Adonai: "I will put my Torah within them and write it on their hearts; I will be their God, and they will be my people"* (Jeremiah 31:33 CJB).

"Now, what is the difference between the two Covenants?"

"He says that this time, He will write the Torah on our hearts; He will put it inside us."

"Exactly! So the Father promises a New Covenant with Israel, then just over five hundred years later He pours out the Holy Spirit on Jerusalem, after Yeshua's death and resurrection, of course. He promises in this Covenant to write the Torah, His Law, on the hearts of His people.

"Does it make any sense at all that one of the first things He commands His fiery new Jewish devotees to do is to delete the fourth commandment—one that has just been written on their hearts, 'Remember the Sabbath day by keeping it holy' (Exod. 20:8), and replace it with something that centuries later, Gentile believers would use in order to excommunicate not only Jews from their communities, but also Gentiles who sought to honor the Jewish Sabbath?"

"It would be highly unlikely," I agreed.

"Another passage people use to say God has changed the Sabbath is Acts 20." *D'ling.*

> *On the first day of the week we came together to break bread. Paul spoke to the people and, because*

he intended to leave the next day, kept on talking until midnight (Acts 20:7).

"First of all, it does not say that it was their custom to meet on the first day of the week, just that they were meeting. Toma already told us that in Jerusalem they were meeting every day. And it is quite possible they had gathered in order to hear Paul, who was their honored guest, speak.

"But even if this were their normal time to meet, let's think it through. They came together on the first day of the week to break bread. The idea is that believers chose Sunday because of the resurrection. So, assuming that they had their worship service in the morning as He rose 'early on the first day,' that would mean Paul spoke from breakfast until midnight! It is highly unlikely that Paul either spoke that long or that they listened that long!"

"Why don't you let me tell you how it was?" another personality emerged from the larger tablet. "My name is Eutychus and I was there. If you keep reading the passage you'll find out that I died—yeah, I really did. I fell right out of a window. Fortunately, Paul was there with the faith to raise me from the dead. The meeting had gone on for hours and I found myself nodding off a few times and then I must have fallen backward, out the window to the ground. Probably wasn't the wisest place to sit. The next thing I know, I am waking up on the ground and Rabbi Saul has his arms around me, praying for me and telling me, 'Don't be alarmed.' Try not to be alarmed when you have just fallen three floors to the ground with enough force to kill you."

"Eutychus, I think you were going to share something with us about the Sabbath," Ariel reminded him.

"I was and I will. David, when does the Jewish Sabbath start?"

"Friday evening."

"So when does it end?"

"Saturday at sunset."

"So when does a new week start?"

I was about to say Sunday, when I realized his point. "Ah, Saturday night."

"You're catching on. So doesn't it make sense that when Luke wrote in Greek, the 'first day,' he really meant, the end of the Sabbath? Jewish believers still went to synagogue on Saturday morning to hear the Scriptures read. Remember, people didn't have Bibles back then, and a good number of us didn't read. The New Testament had not been written! So we were dependent on the Jewish believers to tell us what was written in the Hebrew Scriptures. Then in the evening, as the new week began, we would all break bread together, worship and hear the Word taught."

"That makes much more sense," I agreed. "In Judaism, the day always begins at sunset. We always celebrate the beginning of Jewish holidays in the evening.

"I remember back to the month I spent in Israel during college and how weird it was for me that the week began on Saturday night. When you would see people on Saturday morning, you would greet them with the words *Shabbat Shalom*. However, if you did that on Saturday night, people would think you were strange. The Sabbath is over—the day is over. On Saturday night when you saw people, you would greet them with the words, *Shavuah Tov*, 'Have a good week.' On Saturday evening in Israel, there was a sense that you had left one season and entered into another. Stores that closed for the Sabbath reopened in the evening. Kids got ready for school, which started on Sunday. A new week was beginning."

"Well, I guess I'm no longer needed. Adios, fellows!" And Eutychus was gone.

"And David," added Ariel, "all the Jewish believers living in Israel in the first century, before the destruction of the Temple, would've been going to work on Sunday morning because, just like in Israel today, the Jewish professional work week began Sunday morning. That would have been a difficult time to meet for a worship service.[1]

"Dr. David Stern—one of the foremost Messianic Jewish scholars and an authority on the Jewish roots of the faith—in his *Jewish New Testament*, translates Acts 20:7 like this: 'On *Motza'ei-Shabbat*, when we were gathered to break bread, Sha'ul addressed them. Since he was going to leave the next day, he kept talking until midnight' (Acts 20:7 CJB).

"*Motza'ei shabbat* refers to Saturday night. *Motza'ei* is the Hebrew verb 'to take out,' meaning that we are 'coming out' of Shabbat.

"You would do well to buy a copy of his translation,"[2] Ariel suggested.

"Why don't you just download it to my tablet and save me some money?" I joked.

"Funny, David," Ariel continued. "Now there is something I want you to be very clear about. The Father has no objection whatsoever to people gathering to worship on Sunday. They can worship on any day they want. No one is saying everyone must assemble for worship on the Jewish Sabbath—that's legalism and will produce death. No, the point I am making is that God has never changed the Jewish Sabbath."

"Why didn't God just say, 'Hey, I want everyone to meet on this day?'" I asked.

"*Because there is no set day for worship!*" Ariel half shouted. "The New Covenant is *purposely* silent on this issue because the Gospel would be proclaimed in many nations and received by many different cultures. Believe it or not, many cultures don't use a seven-day week. Much of the Roman world lived by an eight-day week. However, in 321 CE, Emperor Constantine abolished the eight-day week in favor of the seven-day week. And in some areas of Africa, they still use a six-day calendar. So while the message of the Gospel—that Yeshua, the sacrificial Lamb, died and rose again so the world through Him can receive forgiveness of sins and eternal life—is unchangeable, the day and manner of worship of believers is not *written in stone*...no pun intended. Besides, the Sabbath was not given to the Church, but to Israel.

"The problem is not 'Sunday worship' per se," Ariel continued. "A concerted demonic effort to detach the Church from her Jewish roots has played a significant role in all this confusion. The Council's edict to change the day of worship from the Jewish Sabbath to what some refer to as the Lord's Day, exposed the deep anti-Jewish feelings in the Church which could be seen as early as the second century. This carried the unavoidable consequence of alienating Jewish adherents from joining the Church. It has bred a deep distrust of the Church in the hearts and minds of the Jewish people ever since, covering the truth that the New Testament is as much a part of Judaism as the Torah. Sunday worship and the outright rejection of the

Jewish Sabbath confirmed, in the Jewish mind, Christianity's status as another religion altogether."

"Where does the phrase 'the Lord's Day' come from anyway, if it isn't in the New Testament?"

"Oh but it is, my friend. And I should know; I am the one who wrote it!" The face of an elderly gentleman with a long gray beard took center stage on the screen of the large tablet.

Notes

1. Many scholars do believe that the first followers of Yeshua actually met on Sunday night after work. This is a valid view, and even if it is accurate, it in no way invalidates the Sabbath—in fact, it strengthens it. Why didn't they meet on Saturday morning when they were already enjoying a day off from work? Because they were committed to being in the synagogue or Temple courts worshiping and listening to the public reading of the Word alongside observant Jews. Nevertheless, Saturday night still seems more plausible than Sunday night, as it was already a day off—synagogue in the morning, rest in the afternoon, and then the coming together for worship as believers in the evening.

2. Dr. Stern's translation of the Bible can be read free at: http://www.biblestudytools.com/cjb/.

Chapter Sixteen

MESSIANIC JEWISH ATHEISTS?

"Hello David, my name is John—not the John you met earlier. I wrote of that John and his revelation that Yeshua was the Lamb of God in my account of the life of the Messiah. I am John, the disciple whom Jesus loved. We were very close, actually best friends. Even before I understood who He was, I looked to Him as an older brother—a mentor. After a long night in prayer, He chose me and eleven others to be His closest associates and then He spent the next three and half years training us.

"The amazing thing about the Master is that even though thousands followed Him, He always found the time to be alone with us and focus on our training. Most people, who have even a fraction of the charisma and wisdom of Yeshua, seek to use it to take advantage of people. Yeshua did just the opposite. He shunned popularity and focused on leadership training. We didn't understand it at the time, but He was raising us up to lead the Jerusalem revival once He left. And it could not have been easy for Him.

"We were a quarrelsome bunch. My mother once asked Him if my brother, Jacob, could sit on His right hand and I on his left in the Messianic Kingdom. This led to all kinds of backbiting, gossip, and jealousy among the disciples.

"Meanwhile, He always spoke of being a servant. Yet it wasn't until He washed our feet, just as a servant would, that we finally began to understand. And not a moment too soon, as just a few hours later He was nailed to an execution stake showing us the full extent of His servant's heart.

"I was able, *Baruch HaShem*, to outlive all the other apostles. It wasn't easy, mind you. Emperor Domitian, who hated believers in the Messiah, commanded that I be *boiled alive* in oil! Roman guards seized me in Ephesus and extradited me to Rome. I was nearly ninety years old, in an age when most men barely made it past fifty. And what was my crime? Atheism, of all nonsense!

"I stood before a man who claimed to be God, as they accused me of being a heretic."

"How could you be an atheist? You were a believer," I asked, puzzled. "Goodness, you wrote the book of John!"

"And Revelation and the Epistles, uniquely titled First, Second, and Third John," he added with a smile. "The one religion that covered the entire Roman Empire during those years was Caesar worship. Every emperor after Caesar was thought to be divine. So those who wouldn't worship Caesar were considered atheists or heretics. The punishment for this depended on the ruling emperor of the time. When I was on trial, Domitian was Emperor of Rome. He was referred to in his public documents as *Our Lord and God* and he took his divinity quite seriously. He was one of the most vicious men in history. In 96 CE, he put to death his own cousin for being an atheist. Of course he was actually a believer in Yeshua, but any refusal to worship the emperor as God earned you the title of atheist. And you are going to be amazed at how he came to faith! Just wait."

A quote, though not from the Bible, appeared on my tablet. I was reminded that Ariel had forewarned me that he would be downloading information from a variety of sources.

> He informed all governors that government announcements and proclamations must begin, "Our Lord and God, Domitian, commands"...They must call Domitian God—or die. Thus the issue was clear. It was a matter of gods. Either the Lord Jesus Christ or the Emperor of Rome was Lord-God. It was Jesus or Caesar.[1]

"I was brought before the Emperor to be judged. We were in a full coliseum-turned-courtroom, and he asked me, 'Is it true you are an atheist, and refuse to declare that Caesar is God?'

"I serve Yeshua, the Messiah, the King of Israel, Savior of the world."

"*Whoa!* Dude, that is impressive! What did he do?" I asked.

"He got a little upset." John smiled, clearly understating the event.

"The great Domitian responded," John now assumed a grand imperial tone, "'You understand that the penalty for atheism is death?'

"I was in my eighties, David. What was he going to threaten me with, *Heaven?* I was more than ready to join all my friends who had gone on before me, each one of them dying for the cause. Now it would be my turn, or so I thought. Domitian was, in essence, doing me a favor. I can't tell you that I was too excited about being *boiled in oil*. But David, God will always give us grace for anything He permits. In that moment I thought of Stephen."

"Who is Stephen?" I asked.

"Stephen is one of my heroes. He was one of our disciples in Jerusalem and a true servant. When the first apostles were feeling overwhelmed by all the administrative duties involved in serving such a large and growing body of believers, we appointed a group of godly men as servant leaders who were suitable for the task."

"Like Yeshua, when He washed the feet of the disciples?" I turned to Ariel who smiled and nodded assent.

"Stephen not only served the people with compassion and humility," John continued, "he was also a mighty and effective communicator of the good news. People would listen to him mesmerized at his ability to explain their need for salvation. Through him, God did many mighty miracles. Blind eyes were opened and the lame walked. At the time, the Kehilah was growing rapidly. Even many Jewish leaders had come to faith. Something the Jewish ruling council was none too happy about.

"God was using Stephen powerfully to bring many Jewish souls into the Kingdom. At that time we were only reaching out to Jews—mostly from Jerusalem, but the message of salvation and forgiveness was also touching many Jewish visitors to the Holy City. Stephen had a supernatural power of persuasion that I have not seen since, and being backed up by signs and wonders, opponents found it difficult to argue with him. He was so full of the love of God that many who sought to hate him ended up following Yeshua. He would lead them to Yeshua and then they would return to their hometowns or homelands as believers in their Messiah, taking the good news back with them.

"Some of these Jews who had come to Jerusalem from other countries began to argue with Stephen. They mistakenly assumed that they could easily defeat him in debate, as they were far more learned than Stephen. They were confident that once the bystanders saw how 'baseless' Stephen's arguments were, they would abandon this 'nonsense that the Messiah had come, and had risen from the dead.'

"Well, their scheme didn't go quite as planned. They were the ones who invariably ended up looking foolish as Stephen skillfully countered their every argument. He simply amazed everyone with his quick-wittedness and knowledge. You would have thought he was wearing an earpiece and someone was feeding him the answers. It was as if the Spirit of God was simply telling him what to say. He was a young man speaking to men who were twice his age and who had studied the Hebrew Scriptures all their lives.

"Of course, this is exactly what Yeshua said would happen:

> *Be on your guard; you will be handed over to the local councils and be flogged in the synagogues. On my account you will be brought*

*before governors and kings as witnesses to them and to the Gentiles. But when they arrest you, do not worry about what to say or how to say it. **At that time you will be given what to say, for it will not be you speaking, but the Spirit of your Father speaking through you*** (Matthew 10:17-20).

"Those leaders were flabbergasted and infuriated when they couldn't stand up to Stephen's Holy Spirit-inspired wisdom. So they moved to Plan B. It is amazing to what depths men with wounded egos will stoop. Humiliated by Stephen, they produced false witnesses who accused Stephen of speaking blasphemous words against Moses and against God. This was then reported to the Sanhedrin, the Jewish ruling council, and Stephen was arrested.

When Stephen began to testify in his own defense, the people listened as if entranced. It was supernatural. He stood before those who clearly wanted to kill him, and spoke as if he were an invited guest lecturer. It was obvious to all that he was far more concerned about their well-being and their eternal destiny than he was in defending himself. He used his last chance to defend himself to seek to bring other Jewish men to Yeshua—to salvation.

"It was as though he was seeing deep into the soul of every man there. Take a look."

I did, and saw Stephen testifying before a makeshift court; his face was glowing, like that of angel, as words spilled from his mouth. The members of the Sanhedrin were growing ever more furious. But Stephen, clearly full of the presence of God, was not concerned. He looked up to Heaven and cried out:

"Look, I see Heaven open, and the son of Man standing at the right hand of God."

This so provoked the crowd that with a scream they rushed at him. It was as if the presence of God, which produced such peace in Stephen, had the exact opposite effect on his hearers. They recognized that the more he spoke, the more convincing and powerful he became, but their hearts were so hard; they just wanted to silence him.

They dragged him outside the city and formed a circle around him. Then stones started flying, as one after another hurled rocks at Stephen, gashing his face so badly that blood poured from an open wound on his forehead and from his nose. One missile hit him directly on his left ear, slicing it in half. I could hardly bear to watch as rock after rock found its target. They were killing him. And yet, I couldn't turn away either. Amazingly, despite facing death and being surrounded by a frenzied mob, Stephen remained as calm as any man I had ever seen. No hysterics, no begging for his life. He seemed almost detached...and then I saw why.

As rocks continued to slam him from every direction, he prayed—he actually prayed: "Lord Yeshua," he cried out, "receive my spirit." Then he fell to his knees, and cried out again, one final cry, "Lord, do not hold this sin against them." And he died.[2]

Even in his final seconds, he was more concerned for his killers than himself. I was truly in awe.

I turned to John, "*They killed him!*" he could see the tears in my eyes.

"Actually David, Stephen has never been more alive! When he gave up his spirit, he simply left his body and went to receive his reward. In fact, all of Heaven was cheering when he arrived!"

Notes

1. Patrick M. Jones, *Revelations from Revelation* (Brushton, NY: TEACH Services, 2008), 19.

2. You can read the full account of Stephen in Acts 6 and 7.

Chapter Seventeen

BOILED ALIVE!

"It was that peace that you have just witnessed in Stephen that gave me the courage I needed as I stood before Domitian. I trusted that God's presence would cover me in the same way.

"That demented dictator, Domitian, continued to rant like the madman he was, 'Bow before me, heretic, and declare, "Domitian is god!"'

"I shouted in Hebrew, then in Greek, '*Shema Yisrael Adonai Elohanu, Adonai Echad.*'"

"Hear, O Israel: the Lord our God, the Lord is one," (Deut. 6:4). In English I quoted from memory the Shema—one of the most sacred creeds in Judaism.

"Yes," said John, "and this infuriated him even more. 'Death to the atheist!' he shouted. The crowd joined in. 'Boil him alive! Death to the heretic Jew! Feed his boiled flesh to the lions!' In your day, David, people rail against Hollywood for making ungodly forms of entertainment—and rightly so in most cases. But in my day, there were no movies or reality TV competitions—this was the entertainment. Coliseums would fill to capacity just to watch a man being torn apart by lions, or burned alive or, as in my case, boiled in oil.

"Anyway, as the crowd clamored for my execution or boiling, I stood there enveloped in the peace that passes all understanding and I thought, *This is it. I am finally going to be with Him. Reunited with my best Friend! No more sadness, no more pain, just forever in His presence*—until my thoughts were rudely interrupted by Roman soldiers, men who had been turned into bloodthirsty savages by the inhuman nature of their work, violently grabbing me. They dragged me over to the vat of oil as the crowd followed, eager for a spectacle, and then they hurled me over the top. My body plunged into the massive pot, my eyes closed to keep the oil out, and as quickly as I could, I stood up. The oil, dripping from my head and clinging to my beard, came up to my armpits.

"'Light the fire!' came the command. A flame ignited the dry brushwood beneath the pot. Within minutes I could see tongues of fire rising higher than the massive pot of oil in which I was standing. As the flames burned higher, I knew it would only be a matter of time before the oil would heat up and begin to boil.

"*Time for one last sermon*, I thought, knowing they wouldn't kill me quickly because that would put an end to the show. I opened my mouth, for what I assumed was the last time on earth, and shared as passionately as I knew how about the love of God and His desire that all would be saved. Rather than plead for my life, I exhorted the crowd to turn to Yeshua. 'No emperor can save you. He is not God. No man is divine, but One. Yeshua is the only One who can give you eternal life!'

"David, it simply didn't matter anymore. The worst they could do was kill me, and they were already doing that. I discovered in that moment that when you have nothing to lose, you lose all inhibitions. There's nothing to hold you back. I knew it was my last opportunity in this life, and I was determined to make it count.

"I continued, 'Fear not them that can merely kill the body, but fear Him who can cast both body and soul into hell! (see Matt. 10:28). Turn from your sins and find forgiveness in Yeshua.

"In time, to the delight of the emperor, who I am sure just wanted me to shut up, the oil did begin to boil. David, have you ever been burned by oil?"

"Actually, yes, I have. On my last wedding anniversary, I took my wife to a beach house in Delaware. I had the bright idea of making her dinner—pan-seared tuna. However, I didn't realize how hot the oil had become or what would happen when I placed the fish in the pan. Flames shot up everywhere and boiling olive oil flew out of the pan and onto my hand. For hours my hand throbbed in pain and many months later, I still have the scars on my hand to remind me of it. Of course, that can't be compared to what you went through."

"But still, you have a reference," said John. "You understand boiling oil is lethal. However, even as the oil boiled around me, I felt no pain. In fact, it was just the right temperature—therapeutic even to my old bones!

"Domitian was furious, but the people—they were half terrified, half incredulous. How was it possible? How can a man be put in a pot of boiling oil and survive, and more than that, seem impervious to the experience? Like Shadrach, Meshach, and Abednego, who were thrown into a fiery furnace and were not harmed, I was protected by the Lord. It was quite surreal, to be honest. They threw me in, expecting me to die, but I simply stood there and continued speaking. No burns, no pain...nothing. No one seemed to know what to do. Everyone just stood there staring in confused disbelief. So, finally, I simply climbed out. Even the formerly hardened guards were too terrified to do anything, wondering, *Who is this man? What kind of man could withstand such a lethal punishment?*

"Then I thought, *Well, I'll just leave.* And since no one tried to stop me, that's what I did. I could hear the emperor shouting to his guards to stop me, but they were simply too frightened to respond. I later learned that many who were there that day turned to the faith—*including the cousin of Domitian.*"

"Ah, so that is how he came to believe in Yeshua. And then Domitian later had him executed for being an atheist."

John nodded, "Eventually, because Domitian could not kill me, he had me exiled on the Island of Patmos and that is where I wrote these words."

I heard the familiar sound from my tablet, and read: "On *the Lord's Day* I was in the Spirit..." (Rev. 1:10).

"Many Christians, even some of my own disciples, wrongly assumed that I was referring to Sunday. While I understand why people might assume that, I was actually referring to a specific day of the year on the Roman calendar.

A reference anyone reading the prophecy at the time would have understood.

"As I said, Domitian took the idea that he was deity very seriously. Other religions were tolerated, as long they did not conflict with Caesar worship. This became a problem for the believers as well as for religious Jews who did not believe in Yeshua." Another quote appeared on my tablet.

> Once a year, everyone in the empire had to appear before the magistrates in order to burn a pinch of incense to the godhead Caesar and to say: "Caesar is Lord." ...To refuse to say, "Caesar is Lord," was treason.[1]

"This yearly event was known to be *the Lord's Day*. This is what I was referring to, not Sunday. Believers, knowing my history with the emperor, defying him and surviving, understood the significance of the Lord giving this revelation to me on that specific day. It was meant to highlight the theme of the book of Revelation, which can be found over and over again within it pages: Stand firm in the faith, even unto death. I was chosen to write the book because I had already chosen death over capitulation. In addition to being thrown into a vat of oil, I was on the island because of my faith.

"Consider these verses." *D'ling.*

> *I, John, your brother and companion in the suffering and kingdom and patient endurance that are ours in* [Yeshua], *was on the island of Patmos because of the word of God and the testimony of* [Yeshua] (Revelation 1:9).

*Do not be afraid of what you are about to suffer. I tell you, the devil will put some of you in prison to test you, and you will suffer persecution for ten days. Be faithful, **even to the point of death**, and I will give you life as your victor's crown* (Revelation 2:10).

*To the one who is victorious and **does My will to the end**, I will give authority over the nations* (Revelation 2:26).

*They triumphed over him by the blood of the Lamb and by the word of their testimony; **they did not love their lives so much as to shrink from death*** (Revelation 12:11).

"If anyone is to go into captivity, into captivity they will go. If anyone is to be killed with the sword, with the sword they will be killed." This calls for patient endurance and faithfulness on the part of God's people (Revelation 13:10).

This calls for patient endurance on the part of the people of God who keep his commands and remain faithful to [Yeshua] (Revelation 14:12).

"It was no accident that God chose to give this revelation to me on the very day that virtually every believer under Roman rule—many of them my children in the faith—would be confronted yet again with this crucial test of loyalty: *Caesar or Yeshua?*—a test which for some, could mean death.

"Those believers understood both the reference and its implication."

Another quote appeared on my tablet, "...Many Christians were thrown to the lions, charged with atheism for refusing to sacrifice to the Emperor who claimed to be God."[2]

"You have to understand, David, that to publicly confess, 'Yeshua is Lord,' was to put one's life and family in serious peril. Sadly believers, especially today, miss the point of what my brother, Saul, wrote to the Romans at the seat of Caesar worship: 'If you declare with your mouth, "[Yeshua] is Lord," and believe in your heart that God raised Him from the dead, you will be saved'" (Rom. 10:9).

"That's it? Really? Just confess Him and believe?" I asked.

"Actually, it was a bit more complicated than that for the believers living under Roman rule.

"Once you understand the background of Caesar worship and the persecution it entailed, you suddenly realize that to do this—to publicly confess that Yeshua was Lord—was in essence to say, 'I am willing to die for my faith in Yeshua.' What Saul is doing here is indirectly confronting the issue of commitment, because to confess that you were serving Yeshua was equivalent to confessing that Caesar was, in fact, *not* your Lord. And that could earn you a one-time lunch date with a lion in a Roman coliseum—where *you* were the lunch!

"Still today, believers are suffering for their faith all over the world. In Muslim nations, even nations that tolerate Christianity, they will not allow one of their own to leave Islam. It is a crime punishable by death."

On the board I saw the pictures of two men. One was an African man, the other Middle Eastern. Half of the African man's face was horribly disfigured and his right eye was gone. Under his picture it read:

Umar Mulinde, 38, apostle, Uganda: ex-Muslim who preaches Yeshua to Muslims and supports the state of Israel. Two Muslim extremists threw buckets of acid in his face.

Under the Middle Eastern man it read:

Youcef Nadarkhani, 34, pastor, Iran: ex-Muslim pastor in Iran who was charged with apostasy and sentenced to death. Awaiting execution.[3]

"It saddens me, David, that so many people have missed the central theme of the book, hidden in that verse. The Lord's Day reference was a reference to persecution, something that Youcef and Umar both know well."

"This is fascinating," I whispered, stunned by what I was learning. "So you weren't referring to Sunday at all?"

"No, David, I wasn't. Just think about it. What makes more sense? I am receiving perhaps the greatest prophetic visitation that any human has ever received and I mention—*oh, by the way, it's Sunday.*

"Now, I do understand that Sunday was more significant than Tuesday or Thursday, as Yeshua did rise from the dead on a Sunday, but still, Sunday occurred fifty-two times every year—it wasn't that uncommon. However, doesn't it make more sense that I am referring to the one day of the year when the faith of every believer in the empire would be tested to the hilt, as I am writing a book to encourage them to overcome, persevere, and not give in to persecution?"

"Completely! This is awesome!"

"I am pleased to see that you are grasping this, David. The Master has chosen well."

"Chosen? For what?"

But John was gone. The board was totally blank, but not me. I was high! That is the only word I can think of to describe it. I felt like someone was waking me up, and then I would wake up again, to ever newer levels of knowledge. I don't think there are any words in English to explain it.

"John was amazing, wasn't he?" I rhetorically asked Ariel. "He is my favorite so far. I miss that guy already."

"You can see now why he and Yeshua were so close. Of course He loved them all, but John was a special younger brother in the faith to Him. And David, let me say this one more time before we move on. This is key, and I don't want there to be any misunderstanding. The Lord delights in His people when He is worshiped—no matter what day His people come together to worship Him, and Sunday is just as good as any day. But what I do want you to understand is that Sunday never displaced or replaced the Sabbath. And for Jewish believers in the Messiah, He still expects them to honor the Sabbath—not as a condition to receiving eternal life, but as a matter of identity and calling."

Notes

1. Jones, *Revelations from Revelation*, 19.
2. Ibid.
3. Umar Mulinde and Youcef Nadarkhani are actual 21st-century persecuted believers.

Chapter Eighteen

YESHUA THE LIBERATOR!

"This stuff is so completely Jewish. I can't understand why the Jewish people rejected Him."

"But did they, David? After untold centuries of false doctrines that *authorized* the Church to persecute the Jewish people, it is no wonder that *today* Jews have learned to stay away from the Church. But it was not like that in the beginning. In fact, if the Jewish people had indeed rejected the Messiah, the message would never have been taken to the nations. The fact that *Jesus* is a world-renowned name today and His followers number in the billions is irrefutable evidence of the faith, commitment, and success of those early Jewish believers to whom Yeshua entrusted His message of salvation. It was Jewish messengers who spread His message to Africa, Europe, and Asia.

"Let's go back to the days immediately after Yeshua ascended into Heaven. Take my hand."

We were heading back in time, once again. I loved this part! And again scenes from history flashed below me as we journeyed back through time. When we arrived, it was night.

We gazed once more into the room where Yeshua had celebrated Passover with the disciples. But now the room was filled with men and women who were praying. Ariel began, "Remember, David, how Yeshua, just before He ascended into Heaven, told these people not to return to Galilee but to wait in Jerusalem for what the Father had promised—the Holy Spirit. And as you can see, they are obeying Him even though they don't really know what to expect. They spent their days in the Temple courts and nights back at the Upper Room, constantly seeking God for His promise. There are over one hundred people in that room worshiping Him, and every single one of them is Jewish.

"Let's fast-forward a few days to Shavuot."

And within seconds we were viewing a sea of humanity in the Temple courts on the morning of Shavuot. In one of the enclosures off the courtyard, I could see the 120 gathered here, waiting and praying. This was the same scene he had shown me earlier.

"David, they had no idea what was about to happen. Read this verse." I saw this passage illuminated and read:

> *When the day of* [Shavuot] *came, they were all together in one place. Suddenly a sound like the blowing of a violent wind came from heaven and filled the whole house where they were sitting. They saw what seemed to be tongues of fire that*

*separated and came to rest on each of them. All of
them were filled with the Holy Spirit and began to
speak in other tongues as the Spirit enabled them*
(Acts 2:1-4).

He was filling their mouths with praise and worship and in
a multitude of languages!

We watched, and I was fascinated that it was only the
sound of a mighty wind. There was no movement as the Holy
Spirit visibly fell on each one. It was a sound that could be
heard far beyond the reaches of the place where they were and
the strange phenomenon quickly drew a huge crowd. These
Jews were not only from Israel but from all over the known
world. They had come up to Jerusalem on pilgrimage to celebrate Shavuot.

Imagine their amazement at hearing God's praise going
forth in their own languages. We couldn't help but smile as
we watched Kefa stumble from the enclosure into the Temple court's public area. The Jewish worshipers were staring at
him and the others. Seeing this, Kefa took the opportunity to
explain what was happening. He boldly preached his first sermon under the power of the Holy Spirit to an enormous crowd.

"By the end of the day, David, three thousand men had
believed in Yeshua and were ready to be immersed in water."
(See Acts 2:41.)

"I remember this," I said. "They were immersed in the
mikvot pools surrounding the Temple."

"Let's take a look," Ariel said as he leaned forward, and in
seconds we were watching another amazing scene. There was
great joy amongst the crowd as thousands of new believers

in the southern sector of the Temple were being immersed in water.

"Ariel, that looks like more than three thousand to me!"

"Indeed you are right. They only counted heads of households back then. In truth, there were over ten thousand new believers—and again—all of them were Jewish! And consider, David, many of these men had not traveled with their families. So, while many of them arrived in Jerusalem feeling spiritually broken and beat up, seeking to survive under Roman rule, they returned home as new men. Their wives were stunned as their husbands radiated a new respect and love for their spouses, something that was uncommon in the world at that time.

"Let me take a few minutes to explain something to you and then we will get back to Shavuot. While many people falsely think that the New Testament restricts women, nothing could be further from the truth. Until this time, there had been no document more liberating for women than the New Testament. You have to understand that very few marriages at that time were based on love and mutual respect. Virtually every marriage was arranged. In many cultures women were viewed as property. In Roman cultures women were treated very poorly, often viewed merely as objects for sexual gratification and reproduction. A good many women died in childbirth.

"In richer families, the women were expected to bear children as quickly as possible, with little rest between pregnancies. In fact, many girls were doomed at birth. Boys were preferred, as they could carry on the family name, and for a girl the father would have to provide a dowry to her husband upon marriage. At certain periods in Roman culture, fathers were permitted to *expose* their newborns if they chose. Exposing a child meant that the child was thrown in a river or allowed to die naturally from starvation. This fate, in most cases, fell upon girls."

I was sick at hearing this!

"In most cultures, women could not receive an education, testify in court, socialize in public, or talk to strangers. Young women were usually secluded until marriage and married women, especially in the larger cities, wore veils in public. Men, generally, looked down on women, seeing them as inferior.

"Despite the fact the wives of the Patriarchs are honored in Jewish prayers—Sarah, Rebekah, Leah, and Rachel—it rarely translated into true honor between and husband and wife in the first century. The marriage hardly resembled a modern Hollywood movie, but was a contract between families. I am sure you remember the play *Fiddler on the Roof.* Tevye the Milkman was obsessed with finding suitable matches for his daughters, and that was based on Russia in the early nineteen hundreds. Things have changed rapidly in the last 100 years.

"Yeshua, however, broke all the rules, and treated women as equals in a time when such things were unthinkable. To be clear, we all have defined roles to play in our lives—for instance, you're never going to have baby, David!"

"I hope not!" we laughed.

"The Father has created men and women uniquely different to complement each other in their relationships as they raise families. Men tend to be more disciplinary, while women are more nurturing. Yes, men and women are different, but equally valued and loved by the Father.

"And while on earth, Yeshua frequently challenged the status quo. On His way back from Judea to Galilee, He and His disciples passed through Samaria. While the disciples went into town to buy food, He did the unthinkable. He talked to a woman in public! John recorded the whole story in chapter four of his biography of Yeshua.

"When the disciples came back they were clearly surprised and bewildered to see the Master talking to a woman alone—especially a Samaritan woman!

"Let me show you another example." Ariel snapped his fingers and a portable version of the tablet appeared before me, like a flat screen TV, and a movie began to play.

Yeshua was at the Temple courts teaching a group of eager listeners, when He was approached by an aggressive group of men. They appeared to be religious leaders. Two of them violently pushed a bound woman in the direction of Yeshua. She was scratched and bruised, clearly their prisoner. Her hands were bound. As they pushed her forward, she fell and they made a half circle around her. Then the ringleader turned to Yeshua.

"Teacher, this woman was caught in the act of adultery. In the Torah, Moses commanded us to stone such women. Now what do You say?"

Oh my goodness, they were going to stone her, like they did Stephen. It would have been one thing if this were merely a movie. But Ariel was showing me something that really happened.

"No!" I blurted out. "They can't!" Ariel was smiling. "Ariel, how can you smile? This isn't funny!"

He just looked at me and said, "Keep watching."

I continued to watch, as they asked Yeshua if they should stone her to death. Their accusations and calls for her to be stoned were met with silence. Some of them even appeared to be giddy as they put the weight of this woman's life upon Him.

Yeshua gazed at them intensely, but said nothing. Finally, He bent down and began to write with His finger in the dust on the stone floor.

Ariel interrupted, "David, this was far more than a man writing in dust. In fact, He was essentially saying, 'I am Divine.' It was the finger of God that emblazed the Ten Commandments on the stone tablets. Now here, the Divine Son, humbled by taking on the form of humanity, revealing Himself not as the One who parted the Red Sea or spoke the world into existence, but as a servant, He has a divine message for this woman's accusers."

As he bent down I could see what He was writing, and despite that it was in Hebrew, I understood it. "Pride, deception, manipulation, shame, judging, jealousy...." Even as He wrote they continued to badger Him with questions.

At last, He stood up and, looking them straight in the eye, gently said, "Let the one among you who is without sin be the first to throw a stone at her." And then He resumed writing on the stone floor as they pondered His rebuke. "Lust, greed, hypocrisy...."

His confronters were suddenly very uncomfortable, embarrassed, and clearly outwitted. No one was laughing now as, one by one, starting with the oldest, they all crept away.

Yeshua then untied the hands of the woman. She was weeping, overcome with relief at the sudden change in the course of events. She was sure that stones would soon be digging into her flesh and now she was free. Yeshua asked her, "Where are your accusers? Is there not even one to condemn you?"

"No, Lord," she said.

Yeshua looked at her with eyes of compassion and said, "Neither do I. Go and sin no more."

The tablet went blank.

"You see David, they knew they had no legal authority under Roman law to kill her, and that is why they sought to trap Yeshua. They knew if He said, 'Stone her!' He would be in trouble with their Roman overlords. However, if He was unwilling to pronounce a death sentence over her, they would tell the people that He didn't obey Moses. Instead, He exposed their own sinfulness and guilt. Yeshua, making them look like fools, revealed that their sin was just as evil as hers."

"Is this story in the New Testament?" I asked.

"Yep, that and many more that reveal how counter-culture the teachings of Yeshua were. If you read what Shaul wrote to the Ephesians, it probably won't seem so earth-shattering."

I looked to the tablet and saw: "Husbands, love your wives, just as [Messiah] loved the [Kehilah] and gave himself up for her" (Eph. 5:25).

"That's a beautiful passage," I remarked.

"Sure it is—*for you*—a twenty-first-century American husband. But for the Ephesians and the rest of the known world at the time it was revolutionary. It was not the norm for a husband in those days to regard his wife in this way—as someone to be cherished, protected, someone for whom he would be willing to die. You have no idea how radical this teaching was. Asking a man to express unconditional love and affection for his wife was unheard of. Western culture has Yeshua to thank for this shift. Without the teachings of the New Covenant, the West would never have become as civilized as it has.

"Of course, the belittling and devaluing of women went on for centuries, because the Church did not emphasize these teachings and forbade people to read the Bible for themselves. Even in Jewish circles women continued to be treated poorly. Josephus, the great first century Jewish historian noted, 'The woman, says the Law, is in all things inferior to the man.'[1] Here are a couple more quotes from both Jewish and Christian sources." I looked to the tablet:

> Rather should the words of the Torah be burned than entrusted to a woman...Whoever teaches his daughter the Torah is like one who teaches lewdness.
>
> —ELIEZER BEN HYRCANUS[2]

> What is the difference whether it is in a wife or a mother, it is still Eve the temptress that we must beware of in any woman...I fail to see what use woman can be to man, if one excludes the function of bearing children.
>
> —ST. AUGUSTINE OF HIPPO

"While so much has changed in the West in regard to how women are viewed, much of the world still treats women as objects or property. Hold your stomach and watch this."

A video played on the tablet. A Muslim sheik was teaching on the proper way to beat one's wife. I looked at the angel incredulously. He was not smiling. "If the husband wants to use beatings to treat his wife, he must not do it in front of the children. It must remain between him and her...."[3]

The video ended quickly. "This is sick!" I roared, "Religious leaders giving instructions on the *godly* way to beat your wife!"

"Oh David, if you knew how many horrible and tragic events take place every day on your planet. Women are raped, sold into slavery, and forced into prostitution in nearly every country, every day.[4] Evil men line their pockets with money, as their consciences are seared. They feel no guilt or remorse as they use and abuse these creations of God, whom He made in His image.

"This is why Yeshua was so radical in His treatment of women—He hates the way men have used physical strength to take advantage of women. On another occasion when a woman with a notoriously promiscuous past came and wept at His feet, He did not send her away. He was actually in the home of a religious leader at the time and everyone there judged Him for letting her touch Him. But Yeshua rebuked them. In truth there was no difference between them and her—they were all guilty of sin before God. The only distinction was that the woman recognized she was a sinner, while the smug, self-righteous ones present misguidedly trusted in their own virtue for salvation.

"No one in history has contributed more to the liberation of women than Yeshua," Ariel said emphatically.

Notes

1. Josephus, *Against Apion Book II*, 201.
2. Rabbi Eliezer, "Mishnah, Sotah" 3:4.

3. Wife beating in Islam—The Rules, http://www.youtube.com/ watch?v=Wp3Eam5FX58.

4. The Richmond Justice Initiative (www. richmondjusticeinitiative.com) is a great resource to get educated concerning human trafficking and sexual slavery in the U.S. and around the world. It is headed by Sara Pomeroy, a former student of mine.

Chapter Nineteen

TENS OF THOUSANDS
OF MESSIANIC JEWS

Returning to the subject of the Jewish revival that began on Shavuot 30 CE, Ariel continued, "So these men who were giving their lives to the Messiah returned home as changed men. In most cases, their wives were so affected by the new respect with which they were now treated that they, too, quickly became followers of the Messiah."

I looked at the scene as one after another entered into the mikvot—the immersion pools.

"Rising up out of the water is a picture of the resurrection life—the new life in the Spirit that Yeshua gives to all who ask. And three thousand is a very significant number."

"Why?" I asked.

"Well, Shavuot, traditionally, is the holiday on which Israel celebrates the giving of the Law to Moses at Mount Sinai. On the day Moses brought the tablets of the Law into the camp, the people's sin was so flagrant, Moses threw down the tablets, breaking them—and three thousand men were put to death" (see Exod. 32:19-28).

"So, three thousand people died when the law came, but with the coming of the Holy Spirit three thousand people received new life!" I added.

"Precisely! Shaul wrote to the believers in Corinth, 'He has made us competent as ministers of a new covenant—not of the letter but of the Spirit; for the letter kills, but the Spirit gives life' (2 Cor. 3:6). The letter kills because it only reveals the problem. However, when one receives Yeshua, he now has power to live out God's plan. It was the beginning of a whole new way of relating to God—now the Torah would be written on their hearts.

"And this number quickly grew," the angel continued. "In Acts 4:4 it states that the number of *men* grew to about five thousand—and when you count the rest of the family members that number was closer to twenty thousand, *and*, need I say it...?"

"...*All of them were Jewish!*" I finished his sentence.

"Indeed they were, David, and it wasn't merely the uneducated or the unwanted, though the Lord loves them greatly, who were placing their trust in Yeshua. Acts 6:7 says, 'So the word of God spread. The number of disciples in Jerusalem increased rapidly, and a large number of *priests* became obedient to the faith.'"

"What kind of priests? Catholics?" I asked.

Ariel laughed out loud. "No, there weren't any Catholics yet, David. These were Jewish priests!"

"We have rabbis," I said, "but I have never met a Jewish priest."

"It's true, David. If your typical Jewish person were to read that second part, they would probably all think that these priests were Catholic. Why? Because there is no such thing in modern Judaism as a *priest*. The spiritual leaders in post-temple Judaism are called *rabbis*, which means *teachers*. Without a Temple, last destroyed in 70 CE, there was no need for priests anymore, as the job of the priests was to offer sacrifices to God in the Temple on behalf of the people. Even when there were Jewish priests, they would not have used the word *priest* but *cohen*, which is a common family name even today among Jewish people. The fact that a large number of these men, the *cohanim*, who worked in the Temple had come to faith, shows that the good news of Yeshua was reaching *every sector* of Jewish society."

Ariel snapped his fingers and a rather serious-looking man addressed me from the tablet screen.

"And that included Jewish society outside of Israel as well. Shaul, who once imprisoned Jewish believers, made it a point of principle everywhere he traveled to seek to reach the Jewish people first."

"David, meet Lukas. Everyone up here calls him Dr. Luke."

"Hello, David. What a pleasure to meet you."

Despite his stern demeanor, his voice was warm and his manner friendly.

"Hi...eh...Dr. Luke."

"Dr. Luke was the first historian among the early believers. He traveled with Shaul for some time, always taking notes. Eventually, when Shaul was imprisoned in Caesarea for two years, he began to put together an account of their travels. And he collected information from others, *firsthand accounts*, so he could write a history of the Kehilah, going as far back as the birth of the prophet John. There is no one up here, other than God and Shaul himself, who knows more about Shaul than Dr. Luke.

"I think Shaul would agree that I know more about him than he knows about himself. He was brilliant, but he really could have used a smartphone," laughed Luke. "He was so focused on his task that he would often wear two different types of sandals, forget to eat, or even have his tunic on backward for half a day until someone finally had the courage to tell him. Of course he would always laugh at his absentmindedness. The first thing he would ask me every morning was, 'What city are we in?' It became a running joke between us, even when he was imprisoned for two years in Caesarea, waking up in the same place each morning. The authorities allowed me almost constant access to Shaul during that time.

"But let's talk about Shaul's commitment to reach the Jewish people even while he was called to the Gentiles," said the doctor. Before me lay two passages:

> *I am talking to you Gentiles. Inasmuch as I am the apostle to the Gentiles, I take pride in my ministry in the hope **that I may somehow arouse my own people to envy and save some of them*** (Romans 11:13-14).

> *For I am not ashamed of the gospel, because it is the power of God that brings salvation to everyone*

*who believes: **first to the Jew**, then to the Gentile* (Romans 1:16).

"This next passage may shock you as it did me when I heard Shaul dictate these heartrending words to Tertius, his scribe. We were in Corinth at the time and Shaul was greatly concerned for the believers in Rome. Emperor Claudius had expelled the Jews, both Messianic and non-Messianic, from the city in 49 CE. Midway through the next decade they were allowed to return, however the non-Jewish leaders of the Roman *kehilot* had falsely believed that the exile of the Jews had been a sign that God had rejected them permanently. Upon their return they were treated poorly—as second-class citizens. Much of the book of Romans was written to counter this false theology, with chapters nine through eleven, in particular, being devoted to the topic of God's irrevocable covenant relationship with His people, Israel. And I recall Shaul, weeping unashamedly, sharing God's heart for his brothers after the flesh—Israel."

I speak the truth in [the Messiah]—*I am not lying, my conscience confirms it through the Holy Spirit—I have great sorrow and unceasing anguish in my heart. For I could wish that I myself were cursed and cut off from* [Messiah] *for the sake of my people, those of my own race, the people of Israel. Theirs is the adoption to sonship; theirs the divine glory, the covenants, the receiving of the law, the temple worship and the promises. Theirs are the patriarchs, and from them is traced the human ancestry of the Messiah, who is God over all, forever praised! Amen* (Romans 9:1-5).

I was stunned by what I'd just read. "Yes, David, he was willing to give up his place in Heaven, in the Messianic Kingdom, if by doing so more of his people could know the Messiah and receive eternal life. He carried this burden with him until the end. While false historians have portrayed Shaul as an enemy of Israel, I never met anyone who loved the Jewish people more. Despite his calling to the Gentiles," continued Dr. Luke, "the principle, *to the Jew first,* was always foremost in his mind. Take a look at these passages." Scriptures appeared again as clouds in the air; only this time they were scrolling as I read them. Certain words were in boldface. This was to highlight the fact that Shaul's priority, in every city he visited, was always to seek out the Jewish people and tell them the good news of their risen Messiah:

> *When they arrived at Salamis,* **they proclaimed the word of God in the Jewish synagogues.** *John was with them as their helper* (Acts 13:5).

> *From Perga they went on to Pisidian Antioch.* **On the Sabbath they entered the synagogue** *and sat down* (Acts 13:14).

> *At Iconium* **Paul and Barnabas went as usual into the Jewish synagogue.** *There they spoke so effectively that a great number of Jews and Greeks believed* (Acts 14:1).

> *On the Sabbath we went outside the city gate to the river, where we expected to find a place* [where Jewish people met for] *prayer. We sat down and*

began to speak to the women who had gathered there (Acts 16:13).

As was his custom, **Paul went into the synagogue,** *and on three Sabbath days* **he reasoned with them from the Scriptures** (Acts 17:2).

As soon as it was night, the believers sent Paul and Silas away to Berea. On arriving there, **they went to the Jewish synagogue** (Acts 17:10).

Every Sabbath he reasoned in the synagogue, *trying to persuade Jews and Greeks* (Acts 18:4).

They arrived at Ephesus, where Paul left Priscilla and Aquila. **He himself went into the synagogue and reasoned with the Jews** (Acts 18:19).

Paul entered the synagogue and spoke boldly there *for three months, arguing persuasively about the kingdom of God* (Acts 19:8).

"We see from Acts 14:1, where it says, 'as usual,' and Acts 17:2, which states, 'as was his custom,' that this was something Shaul always did. I was with him during much of this time, and the moment we arrived in a new city, his first question was always, 'Where's the synagogue?' If we'd had a GPS back then, he would have had it programmed to locate every synagogue!

"In many of these places, numerous Jewish people came to faith; in others, there would be persecution. More often than not, it was a mixture of both.

"Everything originates with the Jewish people in God's scheme of things. The Jewish people gave the world the revelation of the one true God, His Word—the Bible—and ultimately the Messiah, Yeshua Himself. In addition to *instant messaging* and *Starbucks*," Luke said with a smile.

Then becoming serious again, he added, "And the children of Abraham have paid a heavy price for being God's chosen vessel—persecution, hatred, even attempted genocide, have pursued them to this day. Without Israel, there is no Messiah, and no salvation. And since the New Covenant was made with the house of Israel and the house of Judah, and salvation is of the Jews, it should come as no surprise that Heaven decreed the good news would be preached to the Jewish people first, and then to the nations. And this proclamation was not without effect! Far more Jewish people than is realized received Yeshua in those first two centuries! And today, again, more and more Jewish people in Israel and all around the world are embracing Him.

"I remember when Shaul returned to Jerusalem," Luke continued. "I believe the year was 58 CE, almost three decades after the birth of the first community of believers. The Gospel by that time had gone all around the known world.

"And surely, you would have thought, by now the Jewish revival in Jerusalem would have died down. But it was not so, David. The movement had continued unabated. When we arrived in Jerusalem, Shaul met with Jacob, the brother of Yeshua and senior leader of the Jerusalem community."

Luke turned to Ariel, "I'm assuming you have explained the Jacob/James name debacle. Such nonsense!"

"Nope, I let Jacob do that himself," Ariel responded with a wink.

"Good. Jacob and the elders," Dr. Luke continued, "gave a great report concerning the work of the Gospel in Jerusalem."

Another verse formed before me.

...Then they said to [Shaul]: *"You see, brother, how many **thousands of Jews** have believed, and all of them are **zealous for the law**"* (Acts 21:20).

"There are two eye-openers here and a mistranslation." I could see that Dr. Luke loved to teach. "First, they report to Shaul that the revival is continuing in power and bearing much fruit. However, it is even better than what you read David, because the Greek word translated "thousands" is *muriades*. Do you know what that word means in English?"

"*Muriades*," I thought aloud. "Clearly, by context, it is an amount. It sounds like *myriads*."

"Right, David. Do you know the meaning of *myriad?*" asked Dr. Luke.

"I don't know. I guess it means *a lot*."

"One myriad is ten thousand. Myriads, plural, are *tens of thousands!*"

A verse formed in front of me as Ariel jumped in, "Dr. Stern's translation of this verse is more accurate."

I read, "...They also said to him, 'You see, brother, how many tens of thousands of believers there are among the Judeans, and they are all zealots for the Torah'" (Acts 21:20 CBJ).

"Not only does Dr. Stern's translation bring out the fact that tens of thousands of Jews or Judeans—Jews who lived in the areas surrounding Jerusalem—had embraced Yeshua, but it suggests something that would have sent shockwaves throughout the Middle Ages during the Crusades and Inquisitions—that these tens of thousands of Jewish believers were 'zealots for the Torah!' Oh, that those so-called Christians who outlawed the Sabbath, forced Jews to deny Judaism and be baptized, among other atrocities, could have simply read this book instead of listening to the lies and half-truths that abounded!

"It destroys the myth that Yeshua came to start a new religion apart from Judaism. Jacob, here, is clearly not reporting this to Shaul as a problem, but as something good. In Yeshua, the Law had meaning. Ezekiel and Jeremiah both prophesied that one day God, who had written His Law on tablets of stone, would one day write it on their hearts!"

> ...I will put My law in their minds and write it on their hearts... (Jeremiah 31:33).

> I will give you a new heart and put a new spirit in you; I will remove from you your heart of stone and give you a heart of flesh. And I will put my Spirit in you and move you to follow my decrees and be careful to keep my laws (Ezekiel 36:26-27).

"Somehow many Christians today have come to look at the Torah, the Law of God given to the Jews, as a bad thing. It was bad only in that it could not produce life—but it was never intended to. The Law itself was given as a revelation of God's righteousness, and thus it exposed man's sinfulness. The Law of Moses not only showed us how to live, it served another role in that it revealed our inability to actually keep the Law—it revealed our need for a Redeemer.

"Shaul, speaking of the Torah in Romans, says: 'So then, the law is holy, and the commandment is holy, righteous and good.... We know that the law is spiritual...' (Rom. 7:12,14).

"These were Jewish believers on fire for God and zealous for the Torah. Now keep in mind, when people today think of the Torah, they often conjure up images of black hats, long black coats, and endless, tedious ritual. Most of modern-day Judaism is not following the Torah per se, but traditions built upon the Torah and a *supposed* secret Oral Law,[1] which Moses was given on Mount Sinai, in addition to the written Law.

"But goodness, what is more *Torah* than the Ten Commandments? Take a look at them—they are God's practical instructions for righteous living, far removed from rote tradition! They are in fact responsible for all that is good in Western civilization. Our constitutions, legal codes, and court systems all find their source in the Law of Moses. The only thing remotely close to ritual is the keeping of the Sabbath, and who can argue with the fact that we all need time off for rest, reflection, and rejuvenation?

"And, David, here is something you may have overlooked. While Shaul had written some of his letters to individual congregations by this time, there was as yet no New Testament. All that the new believers had were the Hebrew Scriptures— the Torah, the Prophets, and the Writings."

"So even the Gentiles of the day were almost solely reliant on the Old Testament?" I asked.

"David—there was nothing else!" Luke asserted. "In fact, when Shaul wrote to Timothy that 'all Scripture is God-breathed,' he was referring to the Old Testament! (See 2 Timothy 3:16.)

"To further illustrate this point, take a look at what Jacob and the other leaders were concerned about." A passage formed as clouds before me.

[The Jewish believers] *have been informed that you teach all the Jews who live among the Gentiles to turn away from Moses, telling them not to circumcise their children or live according to our customs. What shall we do? They will certainly hear that you have come, so do what we tell you. There are four men with us who have made a vow. Take these men, join in their purification rites and pay their expenses, so that they can have their heads shaved. **Then everyone will know there is no truth in these reports about you, but that you yourself are living in obedience to the law*** (Acts 21:21-24).

"Some of the Jewish believers were concerned by rumors that Shaul was teaching a heresy, saying Jews who embraced Yeshua should 'turn away' from the Torah. Furthermore, it confirms that Shaul himself was 'living in obedience to the Law.' The funny thing is the very idea that caused deep concern among the apostles eventually became Church policy in the Middle Ages. The believers were alarmed that Shaul may have rejected the Torah, but by the Middle Ages, not only were Jews who came to faith *not encouraged* to continue to live as Jews, they were *forbidden* to do so! Acts records that Shaul, Jacob, and the other apostles affirmed that it is wrong to teach Jewish believers to forsake Jewish life and calling, but the Church of the Middle Age made it doctrine!

"Some, even today, teach that Shaul left Judaism. But I can show you, just from what I wrote in Acts, that he continued to follow the Torah.

"In Acts 18:18, Shaul cut his hair because of a vow he had taken. What kind of vow do you think would require you to cut your hair?"

"I am not sure." I responded, wishing I had been more attentive in Hebrew school.

"In Numbers 6, Moses receives special instructions for a man or a woman who wants to make a vow of dedication to the Lord. It is called a *Nazirite vow*. During the vow, you would not cut your hair, but at the end of the vow, you would shave your head completely, and Shaul did that.

"Another example is in Acts 27. Let's use Dr. Stern's translation for this: 'Since much time had been lost, and continuing the voyage was risky, because it was already past Yom-Kippur...' (Acts 27:9 CBJ).

"Shaul specifically mentions the Fast, referring to Yom Kippur, the Day of Atonement, here. But why did he not just say, 'because fall had arrived'? Had Shaul truly disassociated himself from Judaism, as some claim, he would not still have been referencing the Hebrew calendar.

"Further evidence is provided when Shaul is on trial in Acts 23:6. He appeals to the fact that he is *a Pharisee and the son of a Pharisee*. Notice he doesn't say that he was, but that he is, as in, 'the present tense,' a Pharisee. People today think the word *Pharisee* means hypocrite, and yet here was one of the most honest, true-to-yourself, theologians in the world saying, 'I'm a Pharisee!'

"Okay. Let's get back to Shaul in Jerusalem; I remember it well! Jacob and the other leaders came up with a plan to show clearly that Shaul continued to live as a Jew. So that everyone would know that he 'was living in obedience to the Law.'

I recorded it in Acts 21. And Shaul, who was nobody's push-over—and I know that better than anyone—went along with the plan just to prove that it was true, that he, while 'not under the condemnation of the Law,' still sought to live according to God's pattern for Israel—the Law of Moses.

"Take it from one of Shaul's closest companions for many years, David. He never stopped living as a Jew."

"Hang on there, Luke. Remember our instructions. Everything must be backed up with Scripture, not commentary. Only then will he be prepared," Ariel interrupted.

"And what do you think I have been doing for the past half hour?" remarked the doctor. "David, I wish you great success on your journey. I trust that something I said will prove useful."

And with that, he disappeared from the screen.

Note

1. The Oral Law or oral tradition is believed to have accompanied the written Torah which Moses received on Mt. Sinai. The Oral Law was supposedly given in order to know how to live out the written Torah. It is believed that Moses passed this down to Joshua and from Joshua to future generations, all the way until it was codified in the Talmud, beginning around 200 CE. However, there couldn't have been an Oral Law because in the time of King Josiah, they had lost the written Law and didn't even know what Passover was, much less an oral tradition. When the book of the Law was recovered, they had to start from scratch. If there had ever been an oral tradition, it had long been gone. Strangely, the Oral Law has now been written down in the Mishna and Talmud. It is probable that the religious Jews in the time of

Yeshua did not actually believe that the Oral Law came from Mt. Sinai, as it was merely referred to as *The Traditions of the Elders*. Yeshua Himself rebuked the Pharisees for putting these traditions above the Word of God (see Mark 7:9).

Furthermore, concerning the idea of an Oral Law, we find in Exodus 24:3-4 that, "When Moses went and told the people all the Lord's words and laws, they responded with one voice, 'Everything the Lord has said we will do.' Moses then wrote down everything the Lord had said...." This passage says that God shared all His laws and Moses wrote them down. There was no secret Oral Law. The children of Israel were told to obey all that was written (see Deut. 30:10; 31:9,24,26; Josh. 1:8). For deeper study on this subject see Michael L. Brown, *Answering Jewish Objections to Jesus: Traditional Jewish Objections*, Volume 5 (San Francisco: Purple Pomegranate, 2010).

Chapter Twenty

BREAKING NEWS!
FIRST-CENTURY
ORTHODOX JEWS PROVE
YESHUA IS MESSIAH

"Wait! Rules? Prepared? Journey? What are you all referring to?"

"Soon, David, soon." Ariel reached for my hand and we
were flying back to the classroom.

Seated at my desk with Ariel standing in front of the massive tablet, he began to sum up this last visit with Luke. "So,
you see, not only was there a massive revival in Jerusalem with
signs, wonders, and miracles, but these Jews continued to live
as Jews. If you had walked up to Yochanan (John), Jacob, Kefa

or any other of the leaders of the Jerusalem revival and said, 'Praise God! How does it feel to be free of the Torah and Judaism and to now be a Christian?' they would have stared at you blankly. They wouldn't have known what you were talking about. All they understood was that they, as Jews, had met their long-awaited Messiah. What could be more Jewish than that? What they may have asked, is, 'What is a Christian?' as they referred to themselves simply as *believers* in those early days. The term *Christian* to describe believers in the Christ, which is merely Greek for Messiah, was first coined by unbelievers many years later, in Antioch, a Greek-speaking city.

"After the Shavuot outpouring, do we see Kefa and John going to a church building to pray? No, of course we don't. Look at your tablet."

I read, "One afternoon at three o'clock, the hour of *minchah* prayers, as Kefa and Yochanan were going up to the Temple..." (Acts 3:1 CBJ).

"They were praying the afternoon *minchah* Jewish prayers," I offered. "Just like I do sometimes at our local synagogue. This is mind-blowing! I never pictured the followers of Jesus praying from the Siddur, the Jewish prayer book."

"Well, the Siddur came later, but make no mistake, they were going to the Temple to pray the afternoon *minchah* prayers. The New Covenant doesn't actually use the word *minchah* in the Greek, but the phrase *the time of prayer,* which for a Jew would have been at three in the afternoon. Clearly they continued in this tradition after coming to faith in Yeshua.

"David, Luke showed you all those passages about Shaul going first to the synagogue whenever he would enter a new city. Do you think he walked in and said, 'Hey, my name's Paul, used to be Saul. Can I share a little bit this morning during the service about a new religion we have started called *Christianity*?'"

"Based on what I learned today, that would be highly unlikely," I admitted, smiling at the very thought.

"Precisely; the Rabbi Shaul's objective was to tell his people that their long-awaited Messiah, the Messiah of whom the prophets of Israel spoke, had come—and that through Him they could have eternal life.

"However David, if you really want to know whether Yeshua was the Jewish Messiah, you don't even need the testimony of Shaul, Kefa, or the prophets. In truth, all you have to do is look to the Jewish leaders of Yeshua's day— the Sanhedrin."

"I don't understand. It was members of the Sanhedrin who handed Yeshua over to the Romans. How could they and why would they prove that Yeshua is the Messiah?"

"Well, they didn't do it on purpose! Watch."

As the tablet flickered and came to life, a scene began to play before me.

I could see a gathering where the high priest, his entourage, and all the Sanhedrin were present. These were the elders of Israel. Then a stunned jailer ran in, shouting, "They're gone! They're gone! Those rebel-rousers have escaped! The jail door was locked and the guards were there, but when we opened it up, they were all gone!"

A buzz traveled throughout the room as the high priest and the captain of the Temple guard tried to figure out what was happening. They were visibly shaken.

Then someone else ran into the room and announced, "The men you put in jail are back in the Temple courts teaching the people!"

Several of the Temple guards went immediately with the captain to investigate. Sure enough, there were Kefa, John, and the others, boldly proclaiming that Yeshua was the Messiah. The captain appeared worried. He could see that the people loved the apostles and what they had to say. If he arrested them by force, the people might revolt. But Kefa and the others simply turned to him and said, "Relax, force won't be necessary. We will come with you."

Once again they were brought before the Sanhedrin. The high priest stood and began to question them in an angry, smug and intimidating tone. "We gave you strict orders not to teach in this name...yet you have filled Jerusalem with your teaching and are determined to make us guilty of this man's blood" (Acts 5:28).

Kefa spoke for the other apostles as he boldly proclaimed, "We must obey God rather than any human authority. The God of our ancestors raised [Yeshua] from the dead after you killed him by hanging him on a cross" (Acts 5:29-30 NLT).

I was reminded again that while the Jewish masses—who came from all over the country to hear Yeshua—loved Him, it was the religious leaders, out of jealousy, who had asked the Romans to execute Him.

"Then God elevated Him to the place of honor at His right hand, as Prince and Savior," Kefa continued with holy boldness. "He did this so the people of Israel would repent of their sins and be forgiven. We are witnesses of these things and so is the Holy Spirit, who is given by God to those who obey Him" (see Acts 5:31-32 NLT).

The high priest and the others were so incensed, they could barely restrain themselves. They wanted to kill the apostles. They were frustrated and jealous that these uneducated Jews from Galilee had the whole city listening to their message. It was clear that they were determined to stop them at any cost, lest they lose their power over the people.

Then one of them, clearly a respected member, stood up. He asked that the apostles be sent outside so they could discuss the issue at hand. Then he raised his voice and said:

> *Men of Israel, take care what you are planning to do to these men! Some time ago there was that fellow Theudas, who pretended to be someone great. About 400 others joined him, but he was killed, and all his followers went their various ways. The whole movement came to nothing. After him, at the time of the census, there was Judas of Galilee. He got people to follow him, but he too was killed, and all his followers were scattered.*
>
> *So my advice is, leave these men alone. Let them go. If they are planning and doing these things merely on their own, it will soon be overthrown. But if it is from God, you will not be able to overthrow them. You may even find yourselves fighting against God!* (Acts 5:35-39 NLT)

Fortunately, his reasoning swayed the majority. The disciples would not be stoned to death...at least, not yet. They were brought in and these arrogant, self-serving demagogues had each of them lashed with a whip and again ordered not to speak in the name of Yeshua. But the apostles, in stark contrast to what you would expect of prisoners who had just been beaten, left rejoicing, and as they did, the tablet screen switched off.

"Wow! What a story. Why does Hollywood waste its time on vampires and Harry Potter? This is far more compelling!"

Ariel asked me, "Do you know the name of the man who stood up and convinced the Sanhedrin not to kill the apostles?"

"No," I answered.

"His name is Gamaliel, remember? I told you earlier that Shaul studied under him. I am sure you have heard of Hillel."

"Of course. He was one of the greatest Jewish scholars ever. Without him, there would be no Mishna or Talmud. Hundreds of universities and every major one in the United States have a *Hillel House*, a place for Jewish students to maintain their Jewish culture and identity while away from home. I would occasionally eat Shabbat meals there when I was in college."

"Gamaliel was Hillel's grandson and also a very respected Jewish voice of his time. He was a senior member of the Sanhedrin. There is no doubt that it was his lineage and respected position that kept the other elders from executing the apostles that day. And what was his argument?"

Like Neo learning martial arts in the Matrix, I could recall everything with vivid detail. "He told them that if Yeshua was not from God, they had nothing to worry about—He would soon be forgotten. That other would-be messiahs had arisen yet they had come to nothing and no one remembered them. However, he warned, if Yeshua was the Messiah then they would not be able to stop His message from spreading and could find themselves in the uncomfortable position of fighting against the very One they claimed to represent."

"Very good, David. Let me ask you something. Did Yeshua's message spread abroad? Do people still follow Him? Do they still talk about Him? Or, like those others, Theudas and Judas, to whom Gamaliel referred, has He been forgotten?"

I didn't even have to answer the question.

"So according to the wisdom of one of the greatest Jewish leaders of the first century, Yeshua must have been sent from God. Amazing! I remember reading, while growing up, that John Lennon once said that The Beatles were more popular than Jesus and that Christianity would eventually vanish."

"Oh, they were popular..." Ariel broke in on my train of thought "...*for a minute*," he said with a hint of angelic sarcasm. "But Yeshua has had staying power for over two millennia. I think it is safe to say that John Lennon had a tendency to *imagine*."

My funny angel.

"You know, David, Orthodox Judaism testifies to the validity of Yeshua's sacrificial death in another quite profound way."

"Really? How so?"

"You are familiar with the *Talmud*, yes?"

"Familiar? I know what it is—the Oral Law written, the *Mishnah* and the commentary on it, called the *Gemara*. But no, I am not a student of it."

"Tell me what you know about Yom Kippur—the Day of Atonement."

"It's the holiest day of the year for Jews. We confess our sins and fast in the hope that God will forgive us."

"Do you sacrifice a goat as well?"

"*No*, what are you talking about?"

"Before *fasting* became the central element on Yom Kippur for the Jewish community, it was all about the sacrifice. Aaron, the first high priest, the brother of Moses, was to sacrifice a goat before the Lord. Actually there were two goats. The second goat was the goat upon which the high priest would lay his hands, placing all the sins of Israel upon it." A passage lit up my desktop tablet:

> *When Aaron has finished making atonement for the Most Holy Place, the tent of meeting and the altar, he shall bring forward the live goat. He is to lay both hands on the head of the live goat and confess over it all the wickedness and rebellion of the Israelites—all their sins—and put them on the goat's head. He shall send the goat away into the wilderness in the care of someone appointed for the task. The goat will carry on itself all their sins to a remote place; and the man shall release it in the wilderness* (Leviticus 16:20-22).

"This is where we get the term *scapegoat*—when someone is made to suffer for, or is accused of, another's crimes."

"Why don't we still do this?"

"Because the Temple was destroyed in 70 CE and all sacrifices ceased. Over time, the emphasis was shifted to fasting, which was also commanded in the Torah, as a sign of acknowledgment of and repentance for sin. But fasting can never take away sin. The whole idea of a sacrifice was that you cannot atone for your own sins and live. That was why a substitute, in this case an animal, had to die in the nation's place—our place."

"So why do we fast then?"

"That's a good question, David. Why *do* you fast?" He paused to give me to time to digest the question and then answered himself, "Imagine that you were caught red-handed breaking the Law. Let's say you were going 100 miles per hour through a busy neighborhood. You are arrested and given a court date. How would you present yourself to the judge? Would you wear torn jeans and a dirty T-shirt before the court?"

"Of course not! I would wear a suit and tie. I would probably get a haircut as well!"

"Why?"

"He is the judge. My fate is in his hands. I would want to communicate to him that I was sorry for what I did in hopes that he would extend mercy. To present myself to him in a disrespectful way would ensure maximum punishment."

"Very good David, but tell me, can wearing nice clothes take away what you did?"

"No, I suppose not."

"In the same way, fasting was never intended to take away sin. It was merely the posture of humility in which the people of Israel presented themselves before the Lord. While the high priest was presenting the offering before the Lord and imparting the sin of the nation onto the scapegoat, the people waited outside in hopes that God would forgive them.

"Now, imagine if, while Aaron was carrying out his ceremonial duties on the Day of Atonement, the people treated it just like any other day—they worked, they ate, they played, they laughed. What would that have communicated to the Lord?"

"That they were not serious or that they didn't even believe they needed to be forgiven," I replied.

"Exactly, but if the people didn't work, or eat, and humbled themselves, that would communicate something entirely different to the Lord. It would convey, 'We are serious. We have sinned. Please accept the sacrifice.'

"And that brings me to my point. Did God always accept the Yom Kippur sacrifices?"

"I don't know. I never really thought about it."

Ariel replied quickly, as if he was eager to share a great insight, "Well, the rabbis and sages over the years thought quite a bit about it! In fact, the Talmud itself, which in the eyes of the Orthodox Jews is equal to Scripture, states as a matter of fact that God rejected the Yom Kippur sacrifices from 30 CE to 70 CE. This can be found in tractate Yoma 39b.

"According to the Talmud, there were several signs that would testify as to whether or not God had received the sacrifice and forgiven the people.

"First, the priest would draw lots from an urn. One of the lots had written on it *LaHashem* or 'For the Lord'. The other lot had the words *LaAzazel*. If the priest drew the lot *LaHashem* in his right hand, that meant that God accepted the sacrifice. However, if it showed up in the left hand, it meant the opposite."

"Well that is just a 50/50 chance. How could the people pin their hopes on such odds? I mean, there is nothing supernatural about that. I could just flip a coin."

"Not so; we are talking the same result over forty years. The chances of flipping a coin just five times in a row with the same result are 3 out of 100! Imagine 40 times in a row!

Believe or not, that could happen only once in 1,099,511,627,776 times—and yet the Talmud claims that it did happen in the first century.

"Another sign was that a crimson thread, which was tied to the horn of the scapegoat, would supernaturally turn white. Actually, part of this thread was taken from the goat and tied to the temple doors. That way the people would be able to see for themselves if it turned white, and this also failed to happen even once during those forty years.

"There were other signs as well. However, the main point is that according to the most respected post-second-Temple period Jewish document—the Talmud—the God of Israel rejected the Yom Kippur sacrifices every year after 30 CE. However, what the Talmud fails to reveal—whether through ignorance or conspiracy—is what took place in 30 CE when God began to reject the offerings."

"The death of Yeshua!" I blurted out.

"Exactly! And of course we know that the reason the counting ended at 70 CE was not because God suddenly began to accept the sacrifices, but..."

"...Because the Temple was destroyed by the Romans!" I finished Ariel's sentence. "There were no longer any sacrifices after that. I never knew this! Jewish people need this information! You are telling me that according to Judaism's most trusted source, from the time of Yeshua's death until the destruction of the Temple, the Yom Kippur sacrifices were not accepted. Unreal!"

"I don't know if you know it, but there are two versions of the Talmud—one, written in Judea called the Jerusalem Talmud and one that was compiled in exile, called the Babylonian

Talmud—and both of them agree on this point." Two passages appeared on my tablet, which I read out loud.

> Forty years before the destruction of the temple, the western light went out, the crimson thread remained crimson, and the lot for the Lord always came up in the left hand... (Jacob Neusner, *The Yerushalmi*, p.156-157).

> Our rabbis taught: During the last forty years before the destruction of the Temple the lot ['For the Lord'] did not come up in the right hand; nor did the crimson-colored strap become white... (Soncino version, Yoma 39b).

"Ariel, the Jewish people—non-religious ones like me, or like I was—don't know this. Someone needs to tell them!"

"Yes, David, someone must tell them, indeed," he stated with a twinkle in his eye.

Chapter Twenty-One

COMMUNION IS JEWISH!

"Come on, David, I want us to return once again to Yeshua's last Passover. It'll be a short visit. Are you up for another flight?"

"You need to ask?" I responded as I stretched out my hand. Instantly we were soaring. As we neared the first century, Ariel began to descend. Live scenes flashed past us as though rewinding a film. The closer we got to our destination, the slower they scrolled. We passed the Day of Shavuot. I could see Yeshua speaking with His disciples. It was followed by a scene where He appeared to a large group of people—more than 500. They were looking at Him in amazement, knowing that this Rabbi had just recently been crucified. Now He was cooking fish on the shores of the Galilee and I could see Kefa jump into the water from a boat and wade to shore. Next, we flew over the open tomb, the rock, and the angels. And finally we returned to the scene of that last Passover.

This is the same room in which Kefa and the other disciples received the Holy Spirit on Shavuot. The meal appeared to be over. Yeshua picked up a piece of unleavened bread, and as He broke it, He said:

> *"Take, eat; this is My body which is broken for you; do this in remembrance of Me"* (1 Corinthians 11:24 NKJV).

Then He shared it with them, each one taking a piece.

"Was that the Afikomen? At our Passover Seder that is the very last thing we eat."

"Keep watching David. I will explain everything in just a minute."

Next, Yeshua picked up a cup of wine and said, "Drink from it, all of you. This is my blood of the covenant, which is poured out for many for the forgiveness of sins" (Matt. 26:27-28) and they drank.

"Wait a minute! Communion was instituted at a Passover Seder? Unbelievable!" I found myself saying that a lot. "When I think of communion, which I hardly ever do, I always envision Roman Catholics lining up to receive a wafer and a sip of wine from their priest. I definitely don't associate it with Passover!"

"David, the blessing of bread and wine has been a Jewish tradition for millennia. You just did not make the connection with the Lord's Supper because the Church has so religisized the practice that it hardly bears resemblance to a Seder meal and the fellowship and warmth of friends sitting around a dinner table. But yes, the Lord's Supper was inaugurated at the last Seder that Yeshua enjoyed before He gave His life as a ransom for all humankind."

"Eh... religisized. Is that a word?"

"I'm an angel. I can make up words. Haven't you ever heard of the tongues of men and angels? Ah, forget it. What I mean is that they so dressed it up in religion, that it hardly resembles its original intent or context. There is so much more I want to unpack with you concerning this subject. I think we need to take this back to the classroom." Ariel's voice trailed off—and this time, instantaneously, I found myself back in my heavenly-ancient-techno classroom.

Ariel just picked up where he had left off, as though we hadn't just traveled two thousand years in time—assuming I was back in the twenty-first century. "During the Passover Seder meal, it is customary to remove the middle piece of the three pieces of matzah from the white linen covering and break it in two. Tell me what happens in your home, David."

"Well, my father, who still leads our Seders, takes his role very seriously, even highlighting in each *haggadah*[1] for every participant (and we usually have around thirty people!) exactly when and where they have to read. He would take one half of the broken piece of matzah, the *Afikomen*, and wrap it in white linen—normally a napkin. He would hide it somewhere in the house and the children would search for it after the meal. The finder would return it to the leader and then we'd all partake of it.

"As a kid, that was the most exciting part of the Seder. My sisters and my cousins and I would run around the house after the meal, tearing our home apart looking for it. The winner got two dollars! Now my girls do the same thing with their cousins, though the going rate is now five dollars." I was smiling. Passover was always a wonderful time in the Lebowitz home. "But what does the tradition of the Afikomen have to do with the Passover? I had never thought to ask."

"The rabbis say it is to remind you of the sacrificial Passover lamb. How right they are! Sadly they don't know who the Lamb is. It can only be understood in light of Yeshua. He was the Lamb of God. He took the matzah, gave thanks and broke it, and gave it to them, saying, 'This is my body given for you; do this in remembrance of me' (Luke 22:19). Clearly the bread He broke was unleavened, as it was Passover. Leaven is often compared to sin in the Bible. Shaul reinforces this when writing to the Corinthians. Read from your tablet."

> *...Do you not know that a little leaven leavens the whole lump? Therefore purge out the old leaven, that you may be a new lump, since you truly are unleavened. For indeed* [Messiah], *our Passover, was sacrificed for us. Therefore let us keep the feast, not with old leaven, nor with the leaven of malice and wickedness, but with the **unleavened bread** of sincerity and truth* (1 Corinthians 5:6-8 NKJV).

"Only Yeshua could say, 'This is My body,' because only He was 'a lamb without blemish or defect' as is stated in First Peter 1:19—He was sinless! Even during the original Passover, the Lord said that lamb had to be 'without defect' (Exod. 12:5). That was because, even though they didn't know it, the lamb pointed to the Perfect Lamb of God, Yeshua."

All these passages were being highlighted on my tablet.

"Amazingly, many churches today serve *leavened bread* for the Lord's supper! They seem to have entirely missed the point that the reason the bread is without leaven is to symbolize that Yeshua was sinless—the only Man without sin.

"Let's listen to how the prophet John, whom you recently met, describes his cousin, Yeshua."

John appeared on the tablet but not in real time, as in our earlier conversation. This was more like watching a video on YouTube. As Yeshua came toward him, John said for all to hear: "Look, the Lamb of God, who takes away the sin of the world!" (John 1:29).

"But in order for Him to be the Passover Lamb," I interrupted, "He would have to—woah—He would have to die!"

"That's right, David. Just like it's depicted in the Seder with the middle matzah, His body was broken. After He was killed, He, too, was wrapped in white linen and hidden for a time. And just as the matzah is found and returned for all to eat, He too returned to life, and those who believe partake of Him."

"This is all so Jewish. I can hardly believe it!"

"It really is! And yet Jewish tradition," continued the celestial professor, "has no clear explanation as to what the Afikomen is, where it came from, or why it is broken. The practice actually predates the first century.[2] This special piece of matzah represented the Messianic hopes of the Jewish people. Even as Moses rescued the children of Israel, the Jewish people looked for the One of whom Moses spoke when He said, 'The Lord your God will raise up for you a prophet like me from among you, from your fellow Israelites. You must listen to him' (Deut. 18:15).

"The Afikomen represented the Messiah. Yeshua, His disciples, and all first-century Jews knew this. When He took the matzah and said, 'Take, eat; this is My body,' let's be honest—it would have seemed very strange if they didn't understand that the broken piece represented the Messiah. However, because they were familiar with the Messianic tradition, they understood His meaning. By taking *that* piece of matzah and saying, 'This is My body,' He was in essence saying, 'I am Israel's Redeemer.'

"Sadly, the rabbis who came after Yeshua sought to disassociate Judaism from the idea that a human being could perform the divine function of redemption. In fact, Moses himself, the central figure of the Passover, was completely removed for this reason! His name is not even mentioned in the Haggadah!"

"That's crazy," I protested. "Of course Moses is mentioned in the Passover Seder—he's the protagonist!"

"Really? Where?" The angel challenged me. And as I thought about it, I realized he was right. I couldn't think of one place in the entire Passover ceremony where Moses was mentioned.

"How can Moses not be part of the Passover celebration? That would be like celebrating the Fourth of July and not mentioning George Washington!" I argued.

"It is all about control, David, and sadly, leaders in virtually every religion do it—whether it is fanatical Islamists telling would-be suicide bombers that they will soon be in paradise, or Catholic bishops creating purgatory in order to raise money for their buildings. They will use any means necessary to keep people from thinking for themselves. However, let's not dwell on that right now, but return to the Afikomen.

"In the Passover, Yeshua, the divine Son, was broken, then wrapped in linen and buried, ultimately conquering death itself, by rising to life.

"The very word *Afikomen* symbolizes the coming of Yeshua."

"What does it mean?" I asked.

"Well, interestingly enough, it isn't a Hebrew word. In fact, it's Greek," the angel explained. "And in the first century it was pronounced in its future tense *Aphikomenos*, which means, 'He is coming!'"

"Amazing. Then there could have been no doubt as to who He was claiming to be!" I exclaimed.

"Of course, there is another equally significant meaning in the hiding of the matzah. Despite being Jewish and coming from Israel, Yeshua has been largely rejected by the Jewish world since the first century. However, the day will come when the Jewish people will return to Him—but only when they search for Him, as children do the matzah."

A passage lit up my tablet and I read aloud, "You will seek me and find me when you seek me with all your heart" (Jer. 29:13).

"You are here today, David, because you chose to seek Him out. But a day is coming when far more than a Jewish writer from Philadelphia will seek Him—all Israel will long for Him. The Father has promised."

Another passage appeared:

> For the Israelites will live many days without king or prince, without sacrifice or sacred stones, without ephod or household gods. Afterward the Israelites **will return and seek the Lord their**

God and David their king. They will come trembling to the Lord and to his blessings in the last days (Hosea 3:4-5).

"But that says they will return to David?" I asked.

"King David was a type of the Messiah, and Yeshua being in the lineage of David was called the Son of David. As you and I know, King David is dead, but Yeshua rose from the dead, and Israel will one day return to Him. In fact, many already have!"

Notes

1. The *haggadah* is a special book which contains not only the story of the Exodus, but the structure and the ritual of the Seder (Seder means "order"). It is read aloud at the Passover Seder.

2. To be clear, there are many valid views on when the *Afikomen* was introduced into the Passover Seder. Some believe it was started by first-century Jewish believers (as it so clearly resembles the Messiah) and was later adopted by the greater Jewish community. The fact that Jewish tradition is so vague and unclear regarding the ceremony lends credence to this view.

Chapter Twenty-Two

THE BLOOD OF THE LAMB ON THE DOORPOST OF YOUR HEART

"Let's move on to the wine," suggested Ariel. "On Passover, Jews drink four cups of wine."

"Right, the Cup of Sanctification, the Cup of Deliverance, the Cup of Redemption and—ah—help me out, Ariel."

"Praise, David, the Cup of Praise."

"Right, the Cup of Praise."

"They each symbolize something powerful. But let's focus in on the third cup, because that is the cup of wine we drink directly after we share the Afikomen—the *Cup of Redemption*. This is the cup that Yeshua took when He said..."

A passage appeared that read, "This cup is the new covenant in my blood, which is poured out for you" (Luke 22:20).

"I get it!" I yelled. "At last, I see it! I don't need to feel guilty because I am Jewish. It is totally Jewish to believe in Yeshua. It couldn't be any more Jewish! He is our Passover Lamb. The perfect, sinless..." My revelation was interrupted by the arrival of another passage on my tablet:

> *For you know that it was not with perishable things such as silver or gold that you were redeemed from the empty way of life handed down to you from your ancestors,* **but with the precious blood of [Messiah], a lamb without blemish or defect** (1 Peter 1:18-19).

Ariel elaborated, "Kefa, after describing Yeshua as the Messiah who would suffer as an innocent Lamb, likens His blood to the blood of the Passover lamb which had to be placed on the doorposts of their homes. His blood would serve a similar, yet even more powerful purpose."

"His blood," I proclaimed, "covers the doorpost of my soul. In the Passover story, the blood of the lamb on the doorpost of one's home kept the Angel of Death at bay. However, Yeshua's blood, and I'm only now just grasping this, protects us for all eternity. The Passover is a picture of what God wants to do spiritually for everyone."

"Right, David!"

"The blood of the spotless Lamb of God is impenetrable. The enemy, Satan himself, cannot touch you once you apply it to your life. It is not merely effective for one special night in Egypt, *but for all eternity.* On that great Day of Judgment, those who believe will be pardoned, exempted from judgment, just as the firstborn male was on Passover, because of the blood of the Lamb."

"Right, David! But there is more. At 9:00 AM, the very hour that Yeshua, the Lamb of God, was nailed to the Cross, the first Passover sacrifices were being offered in the Temple. And when He breathed His last breath and cried out, 'It is finished!' it was 3:00 PM, the exact time of the second Passover sacrifice."

"He truly was the Lamb of God," I whispered.

"And He still is!"

"There is so much more I want to tell you, David, but you must be getting tired by now."

I should have been exhausted, but I was totally alert. "Not at all! *Please*, tell me more!"

"Okay then..." my angel, only too willingly, conceded.

Chapter Twenty-Three

LAMB OR RAM?

Ariel continued, "The Lord laced the Hebrew Scriptures with prophetic hints, pictures, clues, illustrations, and examples, going all the way back to Adam and Eve—all to help us arrive at the truth. Here is one of those hints that points to Yeshua. See if you recognize the story."

In rugged terrain I saw on the larger tablet screen an old man on a donkey accompanied by a young man and his servants. They stopped. The old man was quite obviously giving instructions to his servants who were nodding assent. He seemed to be assuring them that they would return. Then, leaving his donkey with the two servants, he and the young man set off up the mountain. They journeyed together in silence, the young man shouldering a heavy load of wood while the old man bore a heavy heart, but never faltered in his step.

"Is it Abraham and Isaac?"

"Not bad! Now let's listen in." Ariel tapped the massive tablet in the lower right-hand corner and immediately we were able to hear their conversation.

Isaac spoke first, "Father?"

"Yes, my son?" Abraham replied.

"The fire and wood are here," Isaac said, "but where is the lamb for the burnt offering?"

Abraham answered, "God Himself will provide the lamb for the burnt offering, my son" (see Gen. 22:6-8).

I watched as Abraham and Isaac arrived at the place God had showed Abraham and together they built a low altar. And then, after arranging the wood Isaac had carried up the mountain, on the altar, Abraham—*to my shock* (yes, I already knew the story, but actually *seeing* it was different!)—bound his son and laid the compliant boy on the wood.

Was he really going to do it?!

Isaac was clearly confused and questioning, yet without a word he obeyed his father, trusting in his father's perfect love for the son he doted on. Abraham turned away, not wanting Isaac to see the tears which now flowed freely. It was clear that he was struggling with what he knew he must do. I found myself *hoping* he wouldn't do what I already knew he had to do. He turned back to his son and kissed him. His tears falling on Isaac's face and hair, Isaac felt his heart and lungs constrict with fear. Terror gripped him. The unimaginable suddenly became a reality when his father took out a knife!

I wanted to scream, "No. Don't do it!" but I knew it would be to no avail. As Abraham, eyes stricken, raised the knife high to plunge it into his son's heart, suddenly a voice, not mine, was heard.

"Abraham! *Abraham!*" An angel called to him.

His hand frozen in midair, Abraham replied, "Here I am."

"Do not lay a hand on the boy," he said. "Do not do anything to him. Now I know that you fear God, because you have not withheld from me your son, your only son" (see Gen. 22:11-12).

My heart was still pounding. I was actually sweating. I knew the story, but when I saw the knife raised and Isaac tied to the altar, helplessly submitting to his fate, I was beside myself.

"It's okay David..." Ariel assured me. "All this happened a very long time ago. Now focus, David, because I want you to see what's still to come."

I watched as Abraham looked up, but saw no one. He looked around to see who was calling him, but instead saw a ram caught in the thicket. So Abraham sacrificed the ram that God had supplied in place of Isaac, his son. The tablet went into hibernation as the screen went blank.

"Did you see what took place there, David?"

"Yes, he almost killed Isaac!" I blurted out.

"No, David. Something else. Remember when Isaac, on their way up the mountain, asked his father where the sacrifice was? What did Abraham say?"

"He said God Himself would provide a lamb."

"Exactly. So where is the lamb?"

"They found him caught in the thickets," I responded.

"No, David, look at your desktop and read it to me."

"Okay," I looked down and read, "'Abraham looked up and there in a thicket he saw...a *ram*.' Okay, he didn't find a lamb. So? What's the difference?" And then, as if someone flicked on a switch, "Ohhhh!" I said, indicating that I now understood. "Because *Yeshua* is the Lamb!"

"Bravo, David, Yeshua is the Lamb to whom Abraham referred. He didn't know it at the time, but when he said, 'God will provide the Lamb' he was speaking prophetically. And another prophet, John, whom you now know, publically announced his arrival calling Him 'the Lamb of God who takes away the sin of the world.'"

"Yes, I remember!" I exclaimed. "This is amazing."

Ariel continued, "Isaac was a *type* of Yeshua. A *type*, in the Bible, is a person or a prophetic event that predicts or foreshadows something in the future. Isaac, the son of promise, was a prophetic type pointing to Yeshua, who was also a promised Son." A passage popped up on my tablet as I heard the familiar chime.

> For to us a child is born, **to us a son is given,** and the government will be on his shoulders. And He will be called Wonderful Counselor, Mighty God, Everlasting Father, Prince of Peace (Isaiah 9:6).

"Think about it. God had an only Son and Abraham had an only son. Yes, he had Ishmael too, but that had been his own doing. Isaac was the long-awaited *promised* son whose birth was supernatural, in that Sarah was not only barren but far beyond the age of child bearing."

"And Abraham," I jumped in, "was willing to give to God his dearest possession, his only beloved son. In turn, two thousand years later, God reciprocates by providing the Lamb of which Abraham spoke, the One most dear to Him, Yeshua—His only Son!"

D'ling! John 3:16, written in huge letters, filled the screen:

> *For God so loved the world that he gave his one and only Son, that whoever believes in him shall not perish but have eternal life* (John 3:16).

"There were multiple prophecies foretelling just about every aspect of Yeshua's life and ministry. I don't know how anyone could have missed them," Ariel added.

"The problem is that most of us aren't looking. It was only recently that I found myself concerned about the fact that I don't know what God expects from me. I am twenty-eight years old, and this is the first time in my life that I am taking God seriously. I never thought to study the prophecies. I couldn't see what they had to do with me. I think most Jewish people are like me. I am not speaking of Orthodox Jews, but secular, cultural Jews. I mean, my life is good. I make a good living, I am healthy, I love my wife, and have two wonderful daughters. It simply never occurred to me, *until now*, that there might be more."

"Oh David, there is more...so much more," Ariel reassured me. "And it was always there for you, if you had simply searched. For instance, the prophet Isaiah foretold the Messiah's mandate seven hundred years before He came."

The passage from John faded as the prophet Isaiah himself took center screen and began to recite portions from the ancient prophecy. He was clearly well along in years and squinted as he read from a very ancient-looking parchment.

As he read, the passage scrolled across my desktop tablet, with certain words highlighted:

> *Just as there were many who were appalled at him—His **appearance was so disfigured** beyond that of any human being and His **form marred** beyond human likeness—He was **despised and rejected by mankind**, a man of suffering, and familiar with pain.*

> *...Surely he **took up our pain** and **bore our suffering**, yet we considered him punished by God, stricken by him, and afflicted. But he was **pierced for our transgressions**, he was crushed for our iniquities; **the punishment that brought us peace was on him**, and **by his wounds we are healed**. ... And the **Lord has laid on him** the iniquity of us all.*

> *He was oppressed and afflicted, yet **he did not open his mouth**; he was led **like a lamb** to the slaughter, and as a sheep before its shearers is silent, so he did not open His mouth. ...**For he was cut off from the land of the living; for the transgression of my people he was punished. He was assigned a grave with the wicked,** and **with the rich in his death**, though **he had done no violence**, nor was any deceit in his mouth.*

> *Yet it was the Lord's will to crush him and cause him to suffer, and though the Lord makes his life an offering for sin, he will see his offspring and prolong his days, and the will of the Lord will prosper in his hand. After he has suffered, he will*

see the light of life and be satisfied; by his knowledge my righteous servant will justify many, and he will bear their iniquities. Therefore I will give him a portion among the great, and he will divide the spoils with the strong, because **he poured out his life unto death,** and was numbered with the transgressors. **For he bore the sin of many, and made intercession for the transgressors** (Isaiah 52:14; 53:3-12).

As Isaiah disappeared, I protested to Ariel, "But that's not in the Tanach,"[1] I protested, "that's got to be from the New Testament!"

"Look it up for yourself," he said.

"Seven hundred years *before* Yeshua," I pondered aloud. "How could that be? He describes everything!

"He would be rejected. He would suffer for us. He would be sinless and ultimately He would die for us, willingly bearing the punishment for our sins, and then come to life again. But why does it say He would see His *offspring*? Yeshua didn't have children."

"He didn't? There are over one billion people on earth who claim Him as Savior and Messiah. You don't think they qualify as children?"

"Ohhh, I see. It's talking about *spiritual* children!" The familiar chime directed my attention back to the screen. I read out loud: "Yet to all who did receive him, to those who believed in his name, he gave the right to become children of God" (John 1:12).

"And Isaiah also prophesied that He would die a sinner's death—in His case, that was crucifixion, 'He was pierced for our transgressions'—and that He would be buried with the rich. This was fulfilled when Joseph of Arimathea, a wealthy man and a member of the Sanhedrin, the ruling council among the Jews, donated his own tomb for Yeshua's burial. What he didn't know, of course, was that He wouldn't be needing it for long."

"Yeah, because Yeshua would rise from the dead. Like Isaiah said, 'He will see the light of life again.'"

So much! So much to take in! I was finally feeling like I was nearing overload. *Yeshua, the Jew...our elder brother...He was the Passover Lamb...He gave His life willingly for me...like Isaac, He was the Son who was sacrificed...this is it! This is what I have been longing for...this is what has been missing in my li—*

Suddenly, lights and colors were going in every direction, and I was flying out of control, with no angelic escort. "Ariel!" I shouted. Where was Ariel!? *"Ariel!"* I shouted louder.

I was spinning in circles. I was terrified. What was happening?

Note

1. *Tanach* is an acronym for *Torah, Writings, and Prophets.* It refers to the Hebrew Scriptures.

Chapter Twenty-Four

CARRYING HIS CROSS

I hit the ground with a thud and knew somehow that I was back in Jerusalem, *but where?* There was shouting coming from what looked like a palace courtyard. So I walked in the direction of the noise, curious to see what all the commotion was about. As I did so, I felt a strange draft around my legs. Looking down, I saw I was wearing sandals, and...what? *Was I wearing a dress?*

On closer examination, I realized I was arrayed in the typical garb of a first-century Jewish man. Even my arms and legs, I noticed, were darker and hairier. *Sweet*, I thought—this was a nice change from my normal, fair, European-Ashkenazi complexion. Then I had another thought, *How cool would it be if...* I touched my face. Yes! A full beard! Now that was something I could never do before. I was smiling, but not for long.

I walked inside the palace courtyard and standing before a loud and angry crowd was Yeshua, bloodied and bruised, beside someone who looked to be an important Roman dignitary, or ruler.

As I stood there, an order was given and He was taken away by soldiers into the palace, and not gently. I followed behind, amazed at my own fearlessness. The whole company of soldiers surrounded Him. They took His hands and tied them to a post. Another soldier produced a whip that had multiple leather tails, and near the end of each tail were tied lethal shards of lead and glass. *My God! They're going whip Him with that thing!*

Just before they did, everything froze in time and a screen rose up from the ground. It was the size of a widescreen TV. A man appeared on the screen. He was not speaking to me but to a lecture hall of students. He was in his late thirties, and while I was sure he was a Bible teacher, he wasn't dressed in religious attire at all—just jeans, a T-shirt and a sports coat. He didn't talk like a religious person, either. He was a regular guy. I liked him already.

> A flogging was such a barbarous, intense, horrendous mode of suffering that many men simply died from it. They stripped the victim almost naked, which is very shameful in Eastern Jewish ancient culture. The man's neck and shoulders and back and legs and buttocks would be exposed and bare. And on each side would stand a professional executor and he would have

a cat-of-nine-tails. It was a handle from which preceded straps of leather. At the end of each strap was a ball made out of stone or metal and with spikes or bone protruding. The metal would tenderize the man's body and the hooks would sink deeply into the man's flesh.

Then the executioner would take a tug on the cat-of-nine-tails to make sure that the hooks were sunk deeply into the man's flesh. And then he would literally rip the flesh off the man's body. The flesh on the man's back would look like ribbons. He would be a bloodied mess. His body would be absolutely traumatized and thrown into shock.[1]

As the screen retracted I heard a loud *snap!* as the first lash was laid. The sharp and deadly thongs of the whip dug deep into the flesh on Yeshua's back as the soldier violently jerked the whip back, "*No!*" I shouted, but no one heard me, as the crude weapon continued to rip His back apart, as it was laid upon Him again and again. The soldiers were laughing. They were actually enjoying this! Only when the count reached thirty-nine did the torment finally end. Yeshua remained upright only because His arms were tied to the post.

A couple of soldiers went to untie Him. "Smack!" one of the Roman guards struck Yeshua in the face with all his might, drawing blood. The blow was followed by another one, as they continued to goad and mock Him. Yet Yeshua did not retaliate. He just looked at them with compassion. I was stunned. Isaiah's words drifted through my mind as if the prophet were whispering them to me.

He was oppressed and afflicted, yet He did not open His mouth; He was led like a lamb to the slaughter, and as a sheep before its shearers is silent, so He did not open His mouth.

The soldiers then took some thorny branches and proceeded to twist them crudely into a wreath, forming a makeshift crown. As they roughly thrust it upon His head, the long sharp thorns dug deeply into His scalp, causing Him to visibly wince and draw in breath as blood trickled from His punctured brow. Then they covered His nakedness by adorning Him in a purple robe. They began to mock Him, "Hail King of the Jews." Still, He didn't respond.

Those fools! They had no idea that they were beating the very One who gave them life, as again and again, they struck Him over the head and spat on Him. Then, they knelt down before Him in mock homage. Finally, tiring of this charade, they removed the robe and put His own clothes back on His bloodied body. I thought I was going to be sick.

At this point, He was handed over to another garrison who led Him out and laid a heavy wooden cross upon His raw and lacerated back, strapping it to His body. After all this, they were going to make Him carry His own execution stake—the cross on which He was to be impaled! Written on a sign that they would later fasten to the cross were the words, "King of the Jews" in Aramaic, Latin, and Greek (don't ask me how I knew!). The Jewish leaders protested, but the Roman centurion, who appeared to be running the show, refused to have it removed.

Suddenly, they were steering Him in my direction. *Should I run? Should I hide?* But actually, I did neither. I simply froze. A man next to me huddled with his two boys, probably visiting

Jerusalem for the Passover. He certainly hadn't brought them here to see this! They appeared just as stunned as I was.

As they neared, Yeshua collapsed under the weight of the massive cross, slamming His already beaten body against the stone pavement, crushing Him and then pinning Him to the ground. He was physically unable to get up. One of the soldiers started to say something to the man next to me, but when he noticed his sons, he turned to me instead and said something in Greek. Amazingly, I understood him and then realized that the guards had also been speaking in Greek this whole time, and I had understood.

"You! Carry His cross!" He barked at me. Surprisingly, I wasn't scared. I didn't hesitate. I ran to Yeshua and with great exertion, I unstrapped and lifted the heavy beam off His body. It must have weighed well over one hundred pounds. Tears were streaming down my face as this innocent Rabbi lifted His head. His face was half covered in dirt and gravel that now clung to the blood on His check.

And then He looked up at me—or should I say *in me* or *through me. Love* personified gazed into my soul and His eyes penetrated my very being. I felt totally exposed before Him. In that instant, I knew that He knew every wicked thing I had ever done—every time I had secretly looked at pornography, yelled at my wife, or disrespected my parents. He saw. He knew every time I had lied or cheated. He could see every petty grudge I'd ever held, how jealous I was of more successful writers and bloggers, and the pride—oh, the pride of life that consumed me!

In light of what He was suffering, my selfish ambition seemed so absurd. I suddenly felt guilty for joining in with the other students and bullying Rudy Green in Hebrew school. And then, I felt horrible shame for pressuring Beth Sanger to sleep with me in high school, taking her virginity, assessing its value at about the same level as taking a friend's pencil for a test. *What had I done?* I then heard these words in my mind:

> *For the word of God is alive and active. Sharper than any double-edged sword, it penetrates even to dividing soul and spirit, joints and marrow; it judges the thoughts and attitudes of the heart. Nothing in all creation is hidden from God's sight. Everything is uncovered and laid bare before the eyes of him to whom we must give account* (Hebrews 4:12-13).

Laid bare...yes, that was exactly how I felt. He could see everything. I was surrounded by a thousand Roman swords, but the worst they could do was pierce my flesh. The eyes of Yeshua dug deep into the darkest recesses of my soul, leaving me utterly exposed and without excuse.

I thought my heart would burst. I wept for my sin. I wept for those I had hurt. *He* was suffering today for *my* sins. In the past, if I did something that I knew was wrong, I might feel a tinge of guilt, but ultimately would justify my behavior. *What's the big deal? Everyone does it.* Every successive time, it became easier and easier—always less guilt than the time before, and finally—no guilt at all.

Now I was seeing that my sin was indeed a big deal. My sin was doing this to Yeshua. This was not a lamb, bull, or goat at the Temple—this was the Messiah, God's Son, and He was going through this hellish ordeal in order that I might be pardoned! How could I resist love like this any longer!?

Again, I heard Isaiah's voice in my mind:

> *But He was pierced for our transgressions, He was crushed for our iniquities; the punishment that brought us peace was on Him.*

I could not break His gaze. All this time, I'd thought that David Lebowitz was a good guy. *What had I done that was so evil,* I would reason, *I am not as bad this one, or that one.* My problem was that I only compared myself to those around me—my friends and co-workers. But now, looking into the very essence of righteousness, I realized how desperately short I had fallen. Even my good deeds were invariably motivated by pride and ambition.

Isaiah's voice was almost audible:

> *All of us have become like one who is unclean, and all our righteous acts are like filthy rags; we all shrivel up like a leaf, and like the wind our sins sweep us away* (Isaiah 64:6).

At which point another voice broke into my consciousness:

> *The fool says in his heart, "There is no God." They are corrupt, their deeds are vile; there is no one who does good. The Lord looks down from heaven on all mankind to see if there are any who understand, any who seek God. All have turned away, all have become corrupt; there is no one who does good, not even one* (Psalm 14:1-3).

I was experiencing the rudest of awakenings! I was two thousand years in the past on the dusty streets of Jerusalem, with the dying Messiah only a few inches away. I was seeing myself for the first time and it was true—David Lebowitz was not a good guy at all. He was selfish, petty, unforgiving, and corrupt, just like everyone else. I deserved God's judgment.

Then I heard in my spirit:

Oh, what a miserable person I am! Who will free me from this life that is dominated by sin and death? Thank God! The answer is in [Yeshua the Messiah] *our Lord...* (Romans 7:24-25 NLT).

For what one earns from sin is death; but eternal life is what one receives as a free gift from God, in union with the Messiah Yeshua, our Lord... (Romans 6:23 CBJ).

Yes! He is my only hope. He is anyone and everyone's only hope! Despite His knowing everything there was to know about me, I felt no judgment—only indescribable, unsurpassable love and compassion. Despite all the pain, the beatings, and flogging that He had endured, a slight, but undeniable smile that expressed a brotherly affection that I had never felt before appeared on His face as He looked at me. He seemed to be telling me that everything would be okay. He was actually in control.

Note

1. Material based on information taken from Mark Driscoll, "Jesus Died" (sermon, Mars Hill Church, Seattle, Washington, April 1, 2012), accessed November 20, 2012, http://castroller .com/Podcasts/MarsHillChurch/2831461.

Chapter Twenty-Five

"SURELY, THIS MAN WAS THE SON OF GOD!"

"Ahhh!" I cried out as a big Roman boot found my stomach.

"Get up!" the soldier hissed.

The pain brought me back to the harsh present reality, stealing me from His holy gaze. In fact, had it not been for that Roman boot, I don't think I could have broken away from His stare. While it had only been a matter of seconds, it had felt like eternity. So much had been communicated in that brief fragment of time. With another heave, I shouldered the cross and they marched us a little over a quarter mile, outside the city walls, to the place where they would crucify Him.

I was finally ordered to stop and I lowered the heavy cross-beam to the ground. The dreaded moment had arrived—but just before they would nail Him to the wooden beam, the tablet came forth again from the earth as the young Bible teacher returned on the flat screen. Everything and everyone around me froze. The teacher said:

> The ancient Jewish historian Josephus called crucifixion the most wretched of deaths. They could hang for upwards of nine days, going in and out of consciousness, stripped almost, or altogether, naked. It was done publicly; it was state-sponsored terror, meant to instill fear in any other would-be lawbreakers. This would be like crucifying people in front of a local mall, or a store or a park, the kind of place where people frequented often and large crowds would gather.
>
> The body is in such trauma and shock at this point that men are weeping; they are in and out of consciousness, and dripping off of their bodies would be tears and blood. For some this was sport. They thought this was entertaining.[1]

The flat screen descended into the earth and the crucifixion began. I wanted to turn away, but I also wanted these soldiers to know that I would be a witness to their vile deed. No, I would watch it all, I decided as a soldier grabbed Yeshua's arm and held it down on the crossbar, while another soldier pulled out a massive nail, resembling a railroad spike—it was at least six inches long—and placed it firmly against the right hand[2] of Yeshua. A mallet was produced and without wasting any time, with a loud grunt, he brought the head of the hammer down firmly on the center of the nail, pushing deep into the center of the Messiah's hand, between two bones. Yeshua winced, but said nothing. Another strike and it appeared that the spike made its way clear through His flesh, into the wood. A few more blows of the hammer and Yeshua appeared to momentarily lose consciousness as His hand was fastened to the wood. And then the other hand was secured to the beam in the same manner.

The soldiers then moved to secure His feet to the vertical beam. They placed one over the other, and then pounded a single nail through the center of His feet, causing agony beyond description. Once done, they levered the cross into position using ropes and dropped it into a hole about three feet deep in the hard ground, jarring Yeshua's entire body. At the sound of the jolt the onlookers involuntarily shuddered, as the impact pushed His body first upward, then downward on the nails through His hands and feet. The pain He felt would have divided time as He hung there between Heaven and earth.

Thankfully, the scene transformed at this point, as I didn't know how much more of that I could watch. The flat screen reemerged and this time the setting was a university lecture hall where a professor was delivering a clinical, forensic analysis of death by crucifixion to a class of students.

> A death by crucifixion seems to include all that pain and death can have of the horrible and ghastly. Dizziness, cramp, thirst, starvation, sleeplessness, traumatic fever, tetanus, shame, publicity of shame, long, continuous torment, horror of anticipation, mortification of untended wounds, all intensified just up to the point at

which they can be endured at all but all stopping just short of the point which would give to the sufferer the relief of unconsciousness. The unnatural position made every movement painful. The lacerated veins and crushed tendons throbbed with incessant anguish. The wounds inflamed by exposure gradually gangrened. The arteries, especially at the head and stomach, became swollen and oppressed with surcharged blood and while each variety of misery went on gradually increasing, there was added to them the intolerable pang of a burning and raging thirst. And all these physical complications caused an internal excitement and anxiety which made the prospect of death itself, of death, the unknown enemy at whose approach man usually shudders most, bear the aspect of a delicious and exquisite release.[3]

Hung completely naked before the crowd, the pain and damage caused by crucifixion were designed to be so devilishly intense that one would continually long for death, but could linger for days with no relief.

According to Dr. Frederick Zugibe, piercing of the median nerve of the hands with a nail can cause pain so incredible that even morphine won't help, "severe, excruciating, burning pain, like lightning bolts traversing the arm into the spinal cord." Rupturing the foot's plantar nerve with a nail would have a similarly horrible effect.[4]

In crucifying someone, one thing is for sure—
no one was concerned with a quick and painless
death. No one was concerned with the preserva-
tion of any measure of human dignity. Quite the
opposite. Crucifiers sought an agonizing torture
of complete humiliation that exceeds any other
design for death that man has ever invented.[5]

As the lecture ended I was returned once again to the most
amazing history lesson I had ever had. I looked at the Man
hanging from the Cross—He was unrecognizable. The flogging alone had bloodied and torn His flesh from His bones.
The beatings and the pulling out of His beard had so ravaged
His face as to make Him unrecognizable. Again I heard Isaiah's voice in my mind.

> *...his appearance was so disfigured beyond that
> of any human being and his form marred beyond
> human likeness...* (Isaiah 52:14).

The soldiers who had removed His clothes before, placing His naked body on the Cross, were now, like this whole
thing was a game, callously casting lots to see who would get
His garments.

I thought of the movie I had seen as a teenager, *The Robe*,
where Richard Burton plays the Roman tribune who not only
oversees Yeshua's crucifixion, but wins His seamless robe.
The robe brings a curse on him until he finds peace in Yeshua.
But this was no movie. I heard a whisper in my mind: "They
divide my clothes among them and cast lots for my garment"
(Ps. 22:18).

Was this also foretold? I wondered.

Some among the crowd cruelly mocked Him. Even pass-ers-by hurled insults, saying, "If You are the Son of God, then prove it. Come down from the Cross."

I remembered the words that Ariel shared with me when he quoted Yeshua: "No one takes my life from me. I give my life of my own free will. I have the authority to give my life, and I have the authority to take my life back again" (John 10:18 GW).

Even some of the religious leaders taunted Him, "He saved others, but He can't save Himself! He's the King of Israel! Ha! Let Him come down now from the Cross, and we will believe in Him," they laughed. The Roman soldiers joined in.

Astonishingly, a man was suffering a torture unlike any-thing I had ever seen and they acted as if it was nothing more than a show. They had no idea who they were messing with! *He should destroy them!* Call down fire from Heaven! My blood was boiling! Don't they know that He is doing this for them!? My anger *at* them was suddenly overridden by my fear *for* them. This was the Messiah, the Son of the living God, they were daring to crucify.

I would find out later that He could indeed have destroyed them. For when Kefa had sought to prevent His arrest in Gethsemane by lashing out with a sword, Yeshua told him: "Do you think I cannot call on my Father, and he will at once put at my disposal more than twelve legions of angels?" (Matt. 26:53).

A couple of soldiers offered Him some vinegar on a sponge to quench His thirst, laughing and mocking as they did so. I didn't know what was in it, but I soon found out, as the screen emerged again. The young Bible teacher was back and this time he shared something that literally made me gag:

> During a trip to Greece, Israel and Turkey, in one archeological dig, we saw seating from an ancient public restroom. And people would sit on marble slabs and water would roll underneath as a sort of shared bathroom. And underneath the seat there was an opening, so I asked one of the archeologists, "What was that for?" They said that the servants would be paid to take a stick with a sponge on the end and use it to clean the person while they were seated upon the toilet. But then they found that as they reused the sponge people would get sick and they would develop infections. So they began dipping it in wine vinegar as an antiseptic to kill the germs.
>
> I literally, in that moment, lost it. I just sat down and started tearing up and fighting back complete weeping. It dawned on me. When they took the stick with the sponge on the end, dipped it in wine vinegar and tried to shove it into the mouth of Jesus on the cross, they used a soldier's ancient toilet brush. It was the kind of thing he had used to clean himself on the battlefield. And he took that and tried to shove it into the Messiah's mouth, to silence and shame Him.[6]

The tablet reentered the ground and I felt nauseated. As they offered Him the vinegar-filled sponge, the soldiers laughed at Him and shouted, "If You are king of the Jews save Yourself."

And then, looking heavenward, Yeshua cried out for all to hear, "Father, forgive them, for they do not know what they are doing."

My God, they have beaten Him, ripped the flesh from His body, hit Him in the head repeatedly, shoved a crown of thorns on His brow and now, hanging from a cross by His hands and feet, in excruciating pain—*He forgives them!*

I began to weep. *Who is this Man who so generously pardons His tormentors?*

His friends and family looked on in utter anguish. His mother, Miriam, being supported by a young man as she sobbed—wait!—he looked familiar. It was a younger version of the old man John I had met earlier. Yes, he'd been at the Passover meal as well. He did say he was one of the original twelve. Standing with them were several other women.

Suddenly darkness came over Jerusalem—and possibly over the whole world. It was around noon on what had just been a cloudless spring day. In a matter of minutes, it became so dark I could barely make out the Cross. Then in my spirit, a voice recited a prophecy.

> *"In that day," declares the Sovereign Lord, "I will make the sun go down at noon and darken the earth in broad daylight"* (Amos 8:9).

My God! It was as if Elohim wanted to reinforce the fact that we were extinguishing "The Light of the World" when we crucified Yeshua.

I looked straight at Him. He was in agony as He hung there. The whole weight of His body was being brought to bear on the single spike driven through the middle of His feet. There was no little platform for Him to stand upon, as has so often been depicted in movies and paintings. No, His full weight came down upon that rusty nail, sending every nerve of His body into spasm.

Every breath brought searing pain, as He had to push up from His feet using only the spike for leverage to inhale, while His back—which was bloodied and raw, the nerves exposed—would drag against the crudely hewn wood inflicting excruciating pain.

It came as no surprise to me, therefore, when I later discovered that the very word *excruciating* is derived from the word *crucify!*

For six endlessly long hours He hung there as a sense of abandonment and desertion pervaded the hearts of those who kept vigil that day. It must have been the middle of the afternoon, as an eerie foreboding hung over the city, that Yeshua emitted an anguished cry in Aramaic, *"Eli, Eli, lema sabachthani?"* Which, translated, is, "My God, my God, why have you forsaken me?" (See Matthew 27:46.)

As I heard these gut-wrenching words, I was engulfed with a feeling of utter despair, of anguish, of horror, and questioning desperation. I didn't just cry, I groaned. Such a feeling I had never imagined possible. Again, I was reminded of what Isaiah had said, "Yet it was the Lord's will to crush Him and cause Him to suffer...."

I yelled out loud, "How? How could this be God's will?"

Again, the prophet's voice: "...and the Lord has laid on Him the iniquity of us all."

I couldn't stop crying. *He was doing this all for me*. He was taking my punishment.

"*You killed Him, David,*" Ariel had said.

I wept for my sin. I hated what I was. I looked up to find the Messiah's glazed eyes resting on me, as He uttered the words, "It is finished," and exhaled His final breath.

At that very moment, the earth shook violently. I could hear the sounds of rocks splitting as the very ground beneath us heaved and cracked. The soldiers, even their commander, seemed to finally understand that they had committed a terrible crime against Heaven. Cries of terror and fear accompanied the awful realization of everyone that they had perpetrated a horrible evil that day.

In the ensuing stillness, the inner conviction that had fallen upon all present was encapsulated in the centurion's solemn summation, "*Surely, this man was the Son of God!*"

Notes

1. Driscoll, "Jesus Died."

2. I understand that there is much debate as to whether Yeshua was pierced in the hands or the wrists. In my research I found strong arguments on both sides, but at the end of the day, who cares? The focus must remain in the fact that He went to the Cross for us. While it is fine, even commended, to study out these issues, to place too much focus on them obscures the greater issue. He died for us. Nevertheless, if you would like to discuss this, please go to http://on.fb.me/itheft.

3. Frederick W. Farrar, *The Life of Christ* (Dutton, Dovar: Cassell and Co., 1897).

4. As quoted in Paul S. Taylor, "How Did Jesus Christ Die?" Christian Answers Network, 2003, http://christiananswers. net/q-eden/jesusdeath.html (accessed August 11, 2012).

5. Farrar, *The Life of Christ*.

6. Driscoll, "Jesus Died."

Chapter Twenty-Six

WAR!

The verdict was out, but even as the centurion pronounced those words, I felt myself being ripped from the scene—pulled back heavenward. However, this was no casual flight through history with my angel—there was *violence* in the air. I was being forcefully pulled back through time. The images I now saw were no longer below, at least not at first, but above.

This was war.

Angelic beings took their stand against one another. I saw one, a general, dressed in battle armor—instinctively I knew his name was Michael. He was tall, and valiant, and he commanded the respect of all. On Michael's side in the battle were orderly rows of huge angelic beings, warrior angels ready to fight for the cause. Thousands lined up; their devotion to Him was evident.

The demons they fought against all had other names connected to regions. A hideous being, equally muscular and grotesque at the same time, was named the Prince of Persia, while another was called Caretaker of Jerusalem.

But the one that really nauseated me was the king of Rome. He was dressed, not in armor, but in religious garb. He was grossly overweight, reminding me of Jabba the Hut of *Star Wars* infamy. He would eat until he would vomit, and then eat the vomit. He seemed to enjoy every form of perverted behavior there was. Their foot soldiers were a disorderly but vicious crew of demons. They would fight with one another for rank, as ego and arrogance governed them, and yet hate and fear bound them together in a perverse unity.

Below them, how far I could not tell, men fought—first with words, manipulation, and deception and then with weapons. The scenes were clearly *parallel*. Whatever war was being unleashed on earth was also being fought in the heavenlies.

Why was I being shown this? I wondered. *And where was Ariel?*

The battles below were not merely military. Multitudes of conflicts were being waged. I saw a white man in Africa. He stood on a large platform before millions of people sharing passionately about the very things I had just witnessed—that Yeshua the Messiah gave His life for them and through Him they could escape God's wrath and have eternal life. Above the preacher, a spiritual battle ensued—demons desperately seeking to maintain their hold on the people, while angelic beings simultaneously fought for their freedom. So many of the people had chains visibly upon them, like prisoners. I could see that even as the war waged above them, smaller demonic entities had their talons buried deep within many of the hearers. Their names were *witchcraft, adultery, bitterness, shame, abuse*, and the like. The forces of God, both angelic and human, were fighting for the souls of men!

One by one, as the people came forward answering the preacher's call, angelic beings would swoop down, like a smart bomb seeking its target, dislodging these demons' hold upon their captives. The people would respond with tears of joy as they discovered their newfound freedom; some were jumping up and down with excitement. The weight of guilt and sin was gone; the demonic control, broken.

What was clear to me in all of this conflict was the centrality and importance of what Yeshua had accomplished in His death. The absolute power of His blood, the blood of an innocent Lamb, to set the captives free and to authorize angelic intervention on behalf of the souls who believed in Him was in evidence everywhere.

It was absolutely clear to me that the critical factor in all of this was the decision of the person to go forward—to believe in the Messiah and accept what He had done for them. At that moment, they became new people—I could see it—delivered out of Satan's cruel domain into the Kingdom of God. I could tell the difference between those whose sins had been taken away by the Lamb's blood and those who were still under Satan's control.

It was evident that there were other spiritual dynamics at work here as well—the words that came from the preacher's mouth were set on fire by God's Holy Spirit and appeared to me as fiery arrows of Life going forth, literally piercing the hearts of his hearers. I remembered what Luke wrote about the Jewish men who heard Kefa—"They were cut to the heart."

Behind the stage were hundreds of people of whom the crowds were completely unaware. They were engaged in a spiritual war, it seemed, crying out to God for the gathered souls to find freedom and salvation. Some were pacing, others were kneeling, but all were praying. These prayer warriors might have been dressed in normal clothes outwardly, but spiritually, I could see that each one of them was fully dressed in battle armor. As their prayers ascended I could see the spiritual atmosphere around the meeting visibly clearing as the enemy was driven back. With some, tongues of fire were released as they prayed; for others their prayers in the form of incense traveled upward toward Heaven making intercession before God. These people *knew* they were at war.

Still, among all the elements at play here—the preacher's words, the angelic intervention, the believers' prayers and the conviction of God's Holy Spirit—I could see that the pivotal factor remained the decision of the individual either to believe and receive the salvation that Yeshua offered or not. Nothing determined the outcome more than that decisive first step toward Yeshua, taken individually by those in the crowd.

This was all absolutely amazing. As I marveled at everything I had witnessed, at what I had been so privileged to see and hear and know, I felt something dark invade my space, and the next thing I knew, I was being ripped away from the arena of spiritual warfare.

Fear filled my consciousness; it was so tangible I could smell it as I spun out of control in utter darkness. I thought I was going to be sick. Then a cold shiver went up my spine as I recognized that I wasn't alone. I was in the very presence of evil.

After several minutes, I found myself back in the classroom, but I was not prepared for what I witnessed there. Ariel was on the ground; a demonic being had his foot on his neck, keeping him from speaking. Other demonic creatures—the most hideous beings I had ever seen—filled the classroom. A horrible stench emanated from them.

One of them began to move in my direction. I was terrified, but had nowhere to run. I was paralyzed with fear. Then, as he approached me he slowly transformed into another being altogether—so beautiful! So attractive! The most appealing creature I had ever seen.

"David," he said in a voice like velvet that brought with it all the comfort of a mother's tender love, "we have come to rescue you. What happened to you today could have destroyed you, your family. Your father..."

Just then Ariel yelled out. I had almost forgotten him as the beautiful being was blocking him from my view, or at least was trying to. "David!" he yelled, "these demons will masquerade as angels of light, but they want to ki..." (see 2 Cor. 11:14). The demon's foot pushed harder against Ariel's throat, silencing him once again. The beautiful angelic creature momentarily reverted back to its former repulsive appearance as he turned in the direction of the demon guarding Ariel and communicated with a look that could have killed. "Keep him quiet you idiot! We don't have much time!"

As he turned back to me, the transformation reoccurred, becoming more angelic with each degree of the turn. Until once again, I came under his hypnotic appeal—an empathetic love that made me want to just melt in his presence. His silken voice and tender tone mesmerized me, draining me of all resistance. I was no longer afraid of him, but drawn to him, as if enchanted by a spell.

"David," his voice seemed to envelop me, "you are safe now. They cannot confuse you anymore. Can you imagine what this foolish decision—to become a *Christian*—would have done to your family? Your father? Embracing Jesus would kill him!"

I felt the worst guilt I had ever experienced—no, *shame* was a more accurate term. He was right. What was I thinking?

"Do you really want to lose your friends, your family, your standing in the community? Do you want to be labeled a fanatic? Do you want your children to be treated as pariahs by other children? Parents would have warned their children to stay away from yours—that is assuming Lisa hadn't left you and taken the kids with her. Of course you wouldn't want to put them through that."

He was right. I didn't.

"And David, let's be honest. There is nothing wrong with you as you are. You're a wonderful person. Sure, you've made some mistakes, but nobody's perfect. God knows that. He made you from dust, after all. He doesn't expect you to be flawless. And the things you've done wrong, you can make up for by simply doing good deeds. Eventually your good deeds will blot out your sins. You don't need someone else to die for you. You can save yourself, David. That is the beauty of truth—it is all up to you. That is the purpose of religion, to give you a way to make up for your misdeeds.

"Your rabbi was right, David. You are a great writer, but you have never studied religion. How could it be that you, in such a short time, should have discovered a truth that your rabbi, who has devoted his entire life to the study of God, hasn't seen? Thousands of years of sages and rabbinical scholars making it clear that Jesus could not have been the Messiah, and you, a novice, figure it out overnight? It's crazy, David. That is *why* you have a rabbi—to lead you and guide you so you will not be deceived.

"David, it is time to go home now. Don't go and throw away all you have on something that's a lie. You have a great life. You are well respected; you have a beautiful family, a good job, and lots of friends. What more do you need? Moreover, your future is bright. You will write books, successful books. Other authors will quote you. I see a Pulitzer Prize coming your way. I can give you all this. You just need to stop pursuing this nonsense that something is wrong with you."

He made so much sense. What had I been thinking? I almost threw my life, career, and family away. I didn't want to lose it all—to be mocked behind my back as some religious fanatic. How horrible it would be to not be welcomed at our synagogue or the Jewish Community Center, where I not only exercise, but lecture every year. We would have had to move. I couldn't imagine raising Hope and Ellie in an environment where they would surely suffer and be rejected—and not for anything they did—but for what I did. What kind of a father was I? How selfish I had been.

I was drifting now—into semi-consciousness, the feeling one gets in the final moments before anesthesia takes effect. Only I wasn't falling asleep—I was enjoying this barely-awake, dreamlike state. It was wonderful. I didn't even need to think, as thoughts were unconsciously being fed to me.

This beautiful creature had saved me. Embracing Yeshua—I mean, Jesus—would have ruined my life. I continued to drift in and out of consciousness, feeling released from all I had been through. My life was fine. I should be happy, not searching for hidden meaning for my existence.

And just like that a wave of guilt came over me as I had a vision of my father. He was weeping and asking, "David, how could you do this to us? How could you humiliate your mother and me like this?" The shame over what I had almost done was overwhelming. "Thank God your grandparents are not alive to see this! They lost everything in the Holocaust and you want to become a Christian?"

Next I saw my wife—she was hurt and angry. "I am not going to be married to a Jesus freak. Just leave!" she yelled as she pointed to the main door of our house where two packed suitcases had already been placed.

In the scene that followed, my rabbi and I were planning a funeral. "David, I told you this Jesus nonsense would kill your father!" Fear gripped my soul. I was coming out of this perfect sleep into a horrible panic. *My father is dead? I killed him?* My heart was racing.

I felt myself, once more, spinning into space.

Chapter Twenty-Seven

ARIEL!

I abruptly woke up. I was back in Starbucks and I was in a panic. Was that a dream? Had it all been a dream? My heart was racing, like coming out of a nightmare. *My father!* I thought, *Oh, thank God, he's not dead. It was all a dream.* I quickly surveyed the coffee shop to see if anyone noticed me. What a strange morning this had been. I just came in to get some work done and somehow I must've dozed off—right in the middle of the café. But what a dream! It was so real, but here I was safe and sound back in the Starbu—*whoa!*

Apparently it wasn't a dream or I hadn't yet woken up yet, I thought, as I was sucked out of my body, like a vacuum was angrily pulling me back into the heavenlies. Once again I was back at the classroom, but the scene had changed dramatically.

Ariel was no longer Ariel, the *professor*, but Ariel, the *warrior*. His muscles were bulging through his battle gear. He was massive and he was determined, and the situation was completely reversed. Ariel now had that same demon, who'd earlier had his foot on Ariel's throat, on the floor and was returning the favor. Gasping in his mighty grip was my once-beautiful "angel," only now exposed for who he really was, a revolting, hideous creature—a demon.

Other equally huge angels filled the room, each in possession of a cowering demon. Apparently reinforcements had arrived after I left.

Ariel looked directly at me. I felt so guilty for ever having doubted him. "David," he said. His voice was the same and yet completely different. The teacher was gone—the general had arrived. "Did you not understand the meaning of the vision? These creatures are deceitful beyond anything you can imagine. They will disguise themselves as truth, but they remain what they are—hideous, conscienceless, fallen angels." The demon attempted to break Ariel's vice-like grip, but was only squeezed tighter for his trouble.

"In the vision, you saw the battle being waged over the souls of men. A man proclaimed the truth while others prayed, but it was only as each one made a decision to trust in Yeshua that freedom came. But make no mistake, David. There is a battle waging over *your* soul, too. The evil powers of darkness will lie and manipulate with guilt and fear to steer you away from eternal life. They are bent on evil and devoid of conscience. They want to take you with them to their final abode—the lake of fire (see Rev. 20:15). They will play on your emotions, pander to your ego, promise you whatever you want, and then reel you in. They are not unlike me in their desire to shape your mind—except I'm offering you life, while they seek your death."

I spoke but no words came out. I cleared my throat and tried again. "But they said my wife would leave me, and Ariel, I saw my father's funeral. The rabbi said that I killed him! I was told I would lose the respect of my colleagues and my friends would all turn on me."

"And they may," Ariel said with an authority that sent shivers down my spine. "And John the apostle was boiled in oil, John the prophet was beheaded, and Kefa was crucified *upside down*. Thousands of others have suffered an equal or worse fate for the Master, and every one of them has received their reward.

"I understand your concerns, David, but you wanted the truth. And tell me, David, was Yeshua not willing to suffer for you?"

A dagger in the gut! Ariel was right. I had witnessed exactly what He did for me. I saw how they tortured Him without mercy. Goodness, I carried His Cross after it collapsed upon His beaten body! He endured all that for me.

Ariel continued, "Recall the vision, David. When did the demons lose authority over the people?"

"When they finally responded to Yeshua," I answered. "The moment they did angels soared down out of Heaven and set them free as demons were dislodged. The blood of the Lamb broke the power of Satan over them."

"Yes, David, remember what you read earlier in the Torah—the life is in the blood.

"As I said, there is a battle waging for your soul right now. The Holy Spirit has people praying for you, people who don't necessarily even know who you are. They are simply praying in obedience to His prompting. That is how we gained the upper hand over these demons today—through the intercession of His people. You can read later how Daniel the prophet prayed and fasted for three weeks, strengthening Michael and his forces so they could defeat the Prince of Persia and deliver a message to the prophet. In your case, their prayers have released an immense portion of prevenient grace[1] in your life. Prevenient grace is what God uses to draw people to Himself. However, most do not receive what you have received, and one day you will give an account.

"But David, after all is said and done, the decision remains yours. It doesn't matter how many people pray for you; if you harden your heart, as you started to do moments ago, you will cut yourself off from this prevenient grace and the convicting presence of the Holy Spirit. As powerful as the blood of Yeshua, the Passover Lamb, is, it is only effective to those who believe—who surrender to God.

"You must decide, young man. Do you want truth, freedom, and eternal life, or the respect of friends, most of whom, by the way, already gossip about you behind your back? Would any of them even come close to doing what Yeshua did for you? Would any of them be prepared to die for you? Would they allow themselves to be beaten or flogged until their backs had been ripped open? Would any of them allow themselves to be tortured to death for you, as Yeshua was?"

The question was rhetorical. *Of course not; no one would ever do for me what He did,* I thought.

"David, you have a window of opportunity. God is drawing you to Yeshua. But if you choose not to respond, then there is no guarantee He will ever draw you again. You may live the rest of your life and never give it a second thought. This demon right here will seek to make sure of that." At which the demon began to struggle again to get free, but could not.

"He and his friends will feed you every lie you want to hear to keep you blinded. Yes, they will promise you the world, even the coveted Pulitzer."

Oh, how foolish I felt! I'd been ready to trade eternal life for temporary fame and the praise of men. Oh, my deceitful pride.

"Yes, David, they will do whatever it takes to keep you lost and blinded to the truth."

"Blinded!" I exclaimed, "That is exactly what I'd been as I drifted out of here before, escorted by, um...him," I pointed to the demon. "Like I was being lulled into a beautiful lie, one that made sense but would keep me from the truth." I turned toward the demon. I was angry, as I understood how he'd sought to deceive me. He hissed at me in frustration, but unlike before, he was now powerless.

"David, once you give your life to Yeshua, you will not have to worry about these demons. Yeshua will give you authority over them. They'll still be around and they'll never give up trying, but you'll trample them under your feet. Most people are terrified of them, but the truth is, this pathetic being is absolutely terrified that you will receive Yeshua, and then use your authority against him."

The defeated demon writhed, furious that his cover was being exposed. Just a few minutes earlier he had been so strong, so confident and convincing. Now he was weak and wretched, even pitiful, in Ariel's tight grip.

"David, it really is time to go home now. Just like in the vision, you have the option—to choose freedom, to choose Yeshua, or you can remain friends with this guy," nodding in the direction of the demon. "Remember, you initiated this when you began your search for the truth. Instinctively, you knew that there must be more. And now that you've found it, you must decide. That part, no one else can do for you. But the moment you choose Yeshua—the moment you confess that you believe, you will know that you are free—just like the Jews in Jerusalem you saw on the day of Shavuot; just like the ones you witnessed in Africa. You will be free...*and you will know it!*"

Almost as if on cue, I felt myself again being sucked back, this time into a tunnel which reverberated with the words: "If the Son sets you free, you will be free indeed...if the Son sets you free, you will be free...if the Son sets you free, you will be...free...free...free..." (John 8:36).

Note

1. Prevenient grace, "is divine grace that precedes human decision. It exists prior to and without reference to anything humans may have done. As humans are corrupted by the effects of sin, prevenient grace allows persons to engage their God-given free will to choose the salvation offered by God in [Yeshua the Messiah] or to reject that salvific offer." Wikipedia.com, s.v. "prevenient grace," http://en.wikipedia.org/wiki/Prevenient_grace (accessed August 11, 2012).

Chapter Twenty-Eight

DECISION TIME!

I opened my eyes and again I was back in Starbucks. Drool from my half-opened mouth was seeping onto the newspaper I'd been reading, the other half of which lay on the floor. I checked the clock. It was 9:30 AM. Only half an hour had passed. The tattooed hipster was gone, the same young lady was working behind the counter, the student was still pecking away at his keyboard, and the couple by the window discussing business was still discussing business. Nothing had changed apart from the fact that a few more people had entered, and no one, seemingly, had noticed the drooling dude, asleep in the corner.

I stood up...and then quickly thought better of it and sat back down, wondering if this journey was truly over or whether I might not find myself at any moment flying or spinning through time again. Like an accident victim slowly beginning to move his hurting limbs to see if anything is broken, I mentally checked myself. What had just happened? Was it real, or just a dream? Dreams do feel real while you are dreaming, but once you are awake, you realize that it was just a dream. Well, I was now awake. So why did my dream still feel entirely authentic?

Did I just watch Yeshua die? Was I really in Jerusalem? And did I just witness an angelic battle over my soul? Was that even possible? Furthermore, did I just spend what seemed like days—though actually, only thirty minutes—with an angel? Or did I imagine it? Did I just doze off and have an incredibly bizarre dream or did I really meet biblical characters? I smiled as I remembered how they'd interacted with me. Am I Dorothy, finally back in Kansas—or in my case, downtown Philly?

Or did God just answer my prayer—my yearning to know the truth?

Well, there was one sure way to find out. I could simply do a little research on the Internet to see if what the angel told me was true. Was Peter really Kefa, was John the Baptist actually Jewish and was he beheaded, and was James actually Jacob? The subjects I could check on were endless. Was the Last Supper actually a Passover Seder? Were there really immersion pools in the Old City of Jerusalem? Were there really tens of thousands of Jewish believers in Jesus in the first century? And how about all that Caesar worship stuff that John talked about? Google and I would clear this up in five minutes.

I bent down and pulled my laptop from my backpack and opened it up, excited to see if any of this was true. As I clicked on my web browser, I heard a *ding*, signifying that I had new email. I immediately thought of the chime that my heavenly tablet made each time a new passage would appear and I smiled, more convinced than ever that this was all some crazy dream. My research could wait a minute, I reasoned as I opened my mail program to see what email had arrived. My heart skipped a beat.

The new email sender's name was *Ariel!*

I nearly fainted. I stared at the screen of my MacBook Air, mouth wide open in stunned disbelief. *Oh...my...God!* I waited a few seconds, just to give my heart a chance to slow down and organize my racing thoughts. Then I clicked on it.

> Shalom D'vid,
>
> I thought you might need this. See attached. We'll be in touch.
>
> Your celestial mentor,
>
> Ariel :-)

Unreal, I thought. *Can't be!* I just sat there frozen; unable to move for about ten minutes. *So, it was real! It was completely and entirely real! And if he was real, then everything he taught me is true. And...that means...Yeshua is real!*

As I emerged from my state of shock, I began to feel that same feeling that I'd sensed earlier with Ariel. It was an amazing feeling, but so hard to put in human terms. Joy like I've never known. Peace that was beyond description. And with it, revelation and understanding!

Yes, I understood why He came, who He was, and why He had to die. I watched Him exhale His last breath. I carried His

Cross! And I witnessed Him ask God to forgive the very ones who were killing Him. And right there in the café, tears began to flow as I thought of my sin, just as they did when He fixed His gaze upon me. But now I knew He would forgive me. I just needed to ask.

Realizing people were beginning to notice my now uncontrollable display of emotion, I grabbed all my stuff and moved to a more private area where I could further digest what had happened and what was happening to me.

As I sat down again, I realized, *Yes, I believe and nothing will ever be the same.* "I believe," I said out loud, and as I did I felt something—*tangible joy*—leapt inside of me. A weight lifted off of me, and I knew I was different.

I remembered what Ariel had said to me just before I left the classroom this last time: "But now, you must decide. The moment you confess that you believe, you will know that you are free—just like the Jews in Jerusalem that you saw on the day of Shavuot; just like the ones you witnessed in Africa. You will be free...*and you will know it!*"

I was, and I did!

I had found what I was looking for—it was Him, Yeshua, the Messiah, the Jew from Galilee. He loved me! He loved me so much that, in all my confusion, He'd sent *an angel* to open my eyes. Love for Him flooded my consciousness. Tears began to well up again. I craved Him; I wanted more. I wanted to see Him again. I wanted to express to Him what I was feeling. And then, suddenly I remembered the attachment with the email. I turned back to my computer and clicked on it. It opened up into some kind of multimedia encyclopedia program. And everything was there—all I'd learned—everything that had been downloaded to my heavenly desktop was now on my earthly one. *Too much!*

Suddenly, I missed Ariel. He rescued me from that slithering, lying demon. Would I ever see him again? I looked down at the email and reread the words, "We'll be in touch." Yes, I would see him again. *I can't wait!* I thought.

I felt so full of love at that moment, I feared I would burst out sobbing right there in the Starbucks. I jumped up, put my laptop away, left the newspaper, and walked quickly to my car. As I got into my Camry, I was again overwhelmed with emotion—feelings I had never known before. I finally did burst into tears. I cried more that day than I think I had in the past ten years. Not since my grandfather's funeral had I been so overcome with emotion. But that was grief; this was something else. I had never been so happy in my life. My name was written in Heaven and I had become a son of God.

After fifteen minutes or so, I finally turned on the ignition and began my drive home, having no idea what the future would bring. I thought of my wife, my girls and, my goodness, my father, the son of Holocaust survivors. How would they react? I would have to keep this quiet for a while—*but how could I?* They will surely notice the change. Either way, eventually I'll have to tell them. But they hadn't had the advantage of time traveling with an angel. They still viewed Yeshua as we had been taught—a Jew, yes, but one who'd started a new religion, a religion that had persecuted our people in the cruelest of ways for centuries. Fortunately, Ariel had equipped me to answer every question.

I turned onto my street. I was still basking in His presence. Tears were still welling up, as I was filled with such gratitude and deep satisfaction. I had never experienced such peace and contentment in all my life. Yet, it made no sense. My life was about to get crazy. When the Jewish community of Philadelphia discovers that *David Lebowitz*—son of Harvey Lebowitz and grandson of Holocaust survivors Tuvia and Edith Lebowitz, the *Philadelphia Inquirer* columnist—now believes that Yeshua is the Messiah, they are *not* going to be happy. And yet, there I was in my car, just as unworried as one could possibly be. While I didn't want to lose any of these relationships—I loved my wife and my parents—I had found the meaning of life. I later found this passage that described perfectly my new willingness to sacrifice everything in order to have my name written in His book of life:

> *The kingdom of heaven is like treasure hidden in a field. When a man found it, he hid it again, and then in his joy went and sold all he had and bought that field. Again, the kingdom of heaven is like a merchant looking for fine pearls. When he found one of great value, he went away and sold everything he had and bought it* (Matthew 13:44-46).

I had found Life itself and He was a Jewish man. I watched Him suffer as no one has ever suffered. Yes, it will be hard, but how can I turn my back on the One who would do that for me? I was willing to lose everything; friends, family, career... if it ever came to that.

And then I heard His voice speaking inside of me.

> *Whoever wants to be my disciple must deny themselves and take up their cross daily and follow me. For whoever wants to save their life will lose it, but*

whoever loses their life for me will save it. What good is it for someone to gain the whole world, and yet lose or forfeit their very self? Whoever is ashamed of me and my words, the Son of Man will be ashamed of them when me comes in mis glory and in the glory of the Father and of the holy angels (Luke 9:23-26).

No, I will never be ashamed of Yeshua, I thought. Then, as if an alarm had just gone off, I suddenly I remembered something. The entire time I was with Ariel, he and others kept telling me that I had a special purpose—a particular task. What is it I am supposed to do? Am I to tell other Jewish people about the Messiah? Will I write books about this? *I am a writer—a trained journalist. Would anyone publish me?*

I chuckled at the thought of asking my Jewish bosses to get behind such a project. Well, whatever His purpose for me was, I was willing. I hope no one will try to boil me in oil. I smiled, knowing that was a very unlikely scenario in Philadelphia, but whatever comes my way, I trust He will give me the strength to deal with it.

Who would have thought when I woke up that morning, with the grand plan of going to Starbucks, reading the paper, and working on my column, that I would meet an angel—not to mention John the Baptist and Shimon Kefa—that I would travel through time and watch Abraham almost kill his son, listen to Isaiah prophesy, and witness the Last Seder and resurrection of the Jewish Messiah? Not to mention, having a ringside seat to the spiritual battle over my own soul and getting a Master's degree in *truth*. Yet, the most amazing event of all that I witnessed was the act of selfless love that divided history, that was planned even before Abraham became father to Isaac—Yeshua's death on the Cross as our Passover Lamb.

As I neared my house, a peace flooded my soul and I recognized that life as I knew it was over. I also knew my quest was over. Ariel was right. The moment I said those words, *I believe*, something changed inside of me. I would later read this passage: "Therefore, if anyone is in [Messiah], he is a new creation; old things have passed away; behold, all things have become new" (2 Cor. 5:17 NKJV).

Yes! I was a new creation! I am sure that if God had opened my eyes, I would have seen an angel swoop down and cut me loose from the darkness I had walked in all my life. Maybe it was Ariel himself—my angel, my teacher, my friend. The blood of the Passover Lamb was now on the doorpost of my soul.

The spiritual battle for my soul might be over, but a new battle was about to commence once it became public knowledge that David Lebowitz was now a friend of Yeshua. I knew my faith could not remain a secret. I had to tell others. I also knew that it would touch every area of my life, from my family to my vocation.

Yes, it was beginning to make sense. God clearly had something special for me to do—an assignment. I again recalled how Kefa and Jacob seemed excited, even honored to meet me. What was this assignment? Something about exposing the *Identity Theft*, the angel said. *All in good time,* I thought. *For now, I just want to enjoy every second of being in His presence.* At that moment, I assumed I would be enveloped in that peace the rest of my life. *I was wrong.*

I turned into my driveway to find my wife, Lisa, frantic, running to the car, tears streaming down her face.

"David, where have you been? We have been calling you! *There's been a horrible accident!*"

CUT OFF FROM MY PEOPLE

"Don't you ever say that you *used to be Jewish! You are still Jewish and always will be!*"

Like an Old Testament prophet, complete with boney finger in my face, Ziva, an Israeli believer, rebuked me, because when I greeted her, I said, "I also *used to be Jewish.*"

I was a brand-new believer and Ziva was the first other Jewish believer I had met. Until this time, I had considered myself cut off from Judaism. It was a painful price to pay (and one I would discover later that I didn't even have to pay!), but Yeshua had radically changed my life and I loved Him for it, no matter what the cost.

Erroneously, I assumed that to believe in the Jewish Messiah was to renounce Judaism—my religion, my heritage, my culture, and my people. The very statement seems strange, right? If He is the Jewish Messiah, why would I consider myself *cut off*? To understand that, you need to know what it was like to grow up Jewish.

Mr. and Mrs. Christ?

"I was about twelve years old when I first learned that Jesus was Jewish," writes Dr. Michael Brown in his book *The Real Kosher Jesus*.[1] In the same chapter he also shares the story of our mutual friend Jeff Bernstein, who grew up thinking that Jesus was the son of Mr. and Mrs. Christ![2]

I can relate to both of their experiences. I too thought for the longest time that Christ was simply Jesus's last name. We are taught, if not directly, that one of the very definitions of being Jewish is that *we don't believe in Jesus*.

I have a strange memory of a phone call I made when I was about ten years old. I saw a sign on a car that read, "I found it!" In fact, if memory serves me correctly, I had seen this phrase in different places around Richmond; however, this time I jotted down the phone number and called it when I got home. I was curious to discover just what he had found.

The person on the other end of the phone was excited to inform me that he had indeed found Jesus. I hung up the phone. Had I been cleverer at the time, I might have quipped, "I didn't know He was lost!"

When I did "find" Him for myself in 1983 as an eighteen-year-old freshman in college, I assumed I had "left" Judaism. I was now a Christian. I didn't like this term, mostly because everyone I grew up with—except for my Jewish friends—claimed to be one and yet it didn't seem like any of them lived like Christians. It didn't take long for me to realize there were *cultural Christians* and *true believers*. There were people who claimed to be Christians because they grew up in homes where their parents told them they were Christians or because they went to a church on Sundays—and there were those who truly had a relationship with the Living God. In fact, growing up, most of the Jews I knew simply defined Christians as non-Jews.

Even though I did not dare call myself a Christian, I was still quite sure I was now separated from my people, my religion, and my heritage—cut off. If there was one thing I had learned growing up Jewish, it was that Jesus and Judaism don't mix! I couldn't explain everything we believed as Jews, but I could sure tell you exactly what we didn't believe! In my mind, I was now outside the camp.

I Am Still a Jew?

However, when Ziva shared those amazing words with me—*You are still a Jew!*—it changed my life! This was a revelation to me. I am still Jewish? I am still part of the people of Israel?

Of course this would have seemed a very strange revelation to the very first followers of Yeshua, whose Jewishness was never in question. They struggled with the question, "Do Gentiles have to become Jewish in order to believe in Jesus?"— not their own Jewishness. (See Acts 10 and 15.)

Ziva also told me of congregations of Jewish believers who met on the Jewish Sabbath and worshiped Yeshua. Again, I couldn't believe my ears. Jewish synagogues where they believe in Jesus? One year later when I walked into Beth Messiah Congregation in Rockville, Maryland, tears filled my eyes as I saw the largest number of Jewish believers I had ever seen worshiping the Messiah.

For a guy who grew up thinking Mary was Catholic, John was a Baptist, Peter was the first Pope, and the New Testament stories took place in Rome, I was stunned. I began to read the New Covenant for myself. The more I read it, the more astonished I became at how *Jewish* it was. This story didn't take place in Rome, there is no mention of the Vatican or a pope, and the word "Christian" can only be found three times in the entire book! These people were not starting a new religion—they were Jews who believed they had found their Messiah.

Moreover, I discovered:

- Jesus's Hebrew name is Yeshua, which means "salvation."

- Mary was an Israelite called Miriam, a Jewish name, like the sister of Moses.

- John was a not Baptist, but a Jewish prophet in company with Ezekiel, Jeremiah, and Isaiah.

- Paul was actually a Jewish rabbi named Shaul.

- Peter was not a pope, but one of the greatest Messianic Jewish communicators in history.

In fact, I was shocked to discover that Gentiles didn't even begin to believe in Yeshua until many years after He was raised from the dead—and virtually the entire early Church was Jewish!

I have a litmus test on how to come to the right conclusion on controversial theological issues. I ask myself a simple question: If I were untainted by either view, and I was given a Bible and locked in a room, what conclusion would I come to? So let's apply that test to the nature of the person of Jesus.

If a Jewish person, unspoiled by the anti-Yeshua bias in modern Judaism, were locked in a room and given the Gospel narratives to read (Matthew, Mark, Luke, and John), would that person come out of that room concluding that Yeshua was a Gentile, anti-Semitic, or the father of a new religion apart from Judaism?

I contend not only would the person not see Him in that light, but the person would fall in love with Him! He or she would see Him as a hero who stood up to the religious establishment of His day (like Jeremiah and the other prophets did) as well as the political rulers, and ultimately demonstrated His love in the greatest way possible. And that is why I wrote this book—to present the real Yeshua, a Jewish Man from Israel, to my people. But not only that! Gentiles have much to unlearn as well.

The Church's guilt in obscuring the Jewish nature of this Man from Galilee is well documented. Church fathers taught their followers the most bizarre and unscriptural doctrines, such as:

- God hates the Jews.

- It is your duty to hate the Jews.

- The Jews are cursed and will never return to be God's people.

- The Church is the new Israel.

- The Jews must suffer as a nation for the killing of Jesus.

- No one can be both Christian and Jew.

They changed the Gospel and they changed the Savior. The tragic result is that Jewish people see Yeshua "through a glass, darkly," but they must see Him "face to face" (see 1 Cor. 13:12). *Identity Theft* seeks to do that; to allow my Jewish brothers and sisters to see Him as He truly is—King of the Jews. And for my non-Jewish brothers and sisters, get ready to meet your Savior in a new and honest way.

I originally wrote this book in three parts. The first was to:

- Show you emphatically that neither Yeshua nor the New Covenant writers ever intended to start a new religion;

- Explore the Jewishness of the first Messianic believers;

- Prove that there has been a demonic conspiracy to rid the New Covenant of its Jewishness—to ethnically cleanse the faith.

The second was to:

- Expose the roots of Replacement Theology— the idea that the Church has replaced Israel as God's chosen, Covenant people;

- Take a look at history and discover how the Jewish identity of the New Covenant was stolen.

And the third was to:

- Share the history of the miraculous return of the Jewish wing, if you will, of the Body of Messiah;

- Reveal how believers can have an impact in bringing revival to the Jewish people and the world and show God's plan for Israel in the future.

Why Jews Are Simply Not Interested

Apart from the issue of sin itself, there are two primary reasons why Jewish people reject the Gospel:

1. The horrible witness of the historic Church toward the Jewish people, which includes the murderous Crusades, forced baptisms, and expulsions from one's country, all which made the Holocaust plausible.

2. The Gospel message presented today has been cleansed of its Jewish roots, so that it appears to the Jew to be altogether foreign to and distinct from Judaism, when in fact it is a Jewish story.

As Messianic Jews, we are often accused of dressing up Christianity in Jewish garb, when in fact just the opposite is true. Messianic Judaism, the faith of the first century Jewish believers, was stripped of its Jewishness in favor of priestly robes of Rome. I wrote *Identity Theft* in the hope that Yeshua, in His truest form, would be presented to the Jewish people.

Enjoy the journey on which you are about to embark.

RON CANTOR

May 9, 2012

Notes

1. Michael L. Brown, *The Real Kosher Jesus* (Lake Mary, FL: Frontline, 2012), xv.

2. Ibid., xvi.

FINAL THOUGHTS

Thank you so much for reading *Identity Theft*. I would love to discuss with you, online, the content or any issues it raised for you.

If you feel that others would benefit from learning the truths found in this story, tell your friends about the book. Share on Facebook and Twitter, and don't forget to include the link to purchase *Identity Theft:* www.IDTheftBook.com.

Like *Identity Theft* on Facebook: www.facebook.com/identitytheftbook.

Alternatively, you can go to www.amazon.com and search for "Identity Theft Ron Cantor" and leave a positive review.

And if through reading *Identity Theft* you came to faith in the Messiah, find a great Messianic congregation or church that loves Israel so you can grow. If you need help, just email me at ron@cantorlink.com.

Thank you again for reading *Identity Theft*. Part 2 is coming.

RON CANTOR

STAYING IN TOUCH WITH RON CANTOR

Ron leads a ministry in Tel Aviv called Messiah's Mandate, the focus of which is:

- Raising up young Israeli Messianic Jews into leadership.

- Organizing outreach trips to revival hot spots in Third World countries (e.g., Nigeria and Uganda) through the Isaiah 2 Initiative. (www.MessiahsMandate.org/Isaiah2) During their last trip to Nigeria, their team of Israeli believers saw 67,000 people make professions of faith. Now, they are planning an outreach to Uganda in 2013.

- Opening the eyes of believers around the world to the Jewish roots of the faith.

Ron is also part of the leadership team of Tiferet Yeshua, a Hebrew-speaking congregation in the heart of Tel Aviv. In addition, he serves Maoz Israel, led by Ari and Shira Sorko-Ram, by writing a regular blog and producing influential and informative videos. Check out www.roncan.net/MAVugT and www.roncan.net/MavMv2.

Ron blogs four to five times a week at RonCantor.com focusing on a number of different areas:

- History of Israel/Palestinian conflict

- Life as a Messianic Jewish immigrant in Israel

- The Jewish roots of the New Covenant

- Teaching to build up your faith

He also posts updates from the Isaiah 2 Initiative.

To be sure of not missing any of Ron's posts, you can subscribe via RSS or email. Those who subscribe will be sent Ron's e-book, *7 Keys to Overcoming Fear*. This book will equip you with the tools you need to take hold of God in any situation. Learn the four words that will keep you from letting others hold you back. Ron also teaches you how to recognize manipulation and intimidation and to crush it. And it's all *free* by just subscribing to RonCantor.com.

ACKNOWLEDGMENTS

There are several people I would like to thank in making this project a reality. Christy Wilkerson was the first to read this manuscript, and alerted me to the fact that it needed work. Pastor Ed Crenshaw added some great insights that I had missed. Wende Carr, living in Beirut, also did a great job of editing and would often send, with her edits, notes of encouragement that she felt that this book was going to have an impact.

However, one person stands out. Susette McLachlan from New Zealand put almost as much time and dedication into this book as I did. She volunteered to edit *Identity Theft* and I don't think she fully understood how deeply she would get involved. This is a better book because of her hard work. She would sometimes stay up all night working on it. Thank you, Susette!

I want to also thank my daughter Danielle who, from the first time she understood I was writing a new book, never stopped encouraging me and showing interest.

Dr. Daniel C. Juster and Dr. Michael L. Brown, both scholars, authors, and personal mentors to me, made valuable contributions in helping me to present what I believe is an accurate portrayal of the first century believers.

I wish to thank Ari and Shira Sorko-Ram who have graciously given me a platform to share my heart through Maoz Israel.

And I would be remiss not to acknowledge the sacrifice of my sweet Israeli wife, Elana. When I made the decision to rewrite this book as a novel instead of a teaching, I had to get it done in a matter of weeks. I disappeared—physically and emotionally. Even during a ministry trip to Germany, Austria, and Switzerland, Elana was often out sightseeing by herself, while I was confined to my hotel room with my MacBook Air. Thank you, sweetheart, for being so patient and understanding. I promise to take you somewhere amazing just as soon this book hits the printing press! I love you!

Lastly, I want to mention my Hero, my Champion, my Source of encouragement and creativity, Yeshua the Messiah, who pursued me when I had no regard for eternity. *Identity Theft* is His story.

ABOUT RON CANTOR

Messianic Jewish Communicator Ron Cantor embraced Yeshua as an 18-year-old, drug-using agnostic. He then attended CFNI in New York, and Messiah Biblical Institute where Ron received his degree. Ron served on the pastoral team at Beth Messiah Congregation in Rockville, Maryland, before heading overseas to Ukraine and Hungary where he and his wife, Elana, trained nationals for Jewish ministry. Ron then served on the faculty of the Brownsville Revival school of Ministry teaching and mentoring young leaders.

Ron travels throughout the U.S. and abroad sharing passionately on the Jewish roots of the New Testament and God's broken heart for His ancient people Israel. Ron has been privileged to take the Jewish roots message to Brazil, Ukraine, Switzerland, France, Russia, Hungary, Israel, Germany, Argentina, and most recently to Uganda and Nigeria.

In June 2003, Ron and Elana returned with their three children to the Land of Israel where they now live and minister. During this time, Ron has served as the associate leader of King of Kings Community in Jerusalem, as well as the interim senior leader. Ron heads the Isaiah 2 Initiative, an Israeli-based vision to see the Good News go forth from Zion to other nations. In their trips to Nigeria and Ukraine they have seen tens of thousands of people profess faith in Yeshua.

Ron also serves with Maoz Israel, blogging and making informative videos about life in Israel. He and Elana are part of the leadership team at Tiferet Yeshua, a Hebrew-speaking congregation in the heart of Tel Aviv. They have three daughters, Sharon, Yael, and Danielle.

Below are the links to social network sites related to *Identity Theft*:

- Join the FB discussion group: www.on.fb.me/itheft

- Like the book: www.facebook.com/identitytheftbook

- IT on Twitter: #IDTheftbook

- Follow Ron Cantor on Twitter: www.twitter.com/RonSCantor

- Friend Ron on Facebook: www.facebook.com/roncan

- Ron's website and ministry in Israel: www.MessiahsMandate.org

- Ron's blog: www.RonCantor.com

Inviting Ron to Speak

If you would like Ron Cantor to come and speak to your conference or congregation, please go to: www.MessiahsMandate.org/invite-ron. Ron makes three trips to the U.S. each year from Israel and would love to minister at your conference, congregation, or event.

Keep up to date on what God is doing in Israel! And get my book, *7 Keys to Overcoming Fear,* absolutely *free* when you sign up for our newsletter at www.MessiahsMandate.org/Updates.

I want to send you my monthly newsletter free of charge so you can:

- Stay informed concerning what is happening in Israel.

- Know how to pray for Israel.

- Continue to grow in your understanding of the Jewish roots for the faith.

When you sign up, in addition to the *free* book, you can also ask to receive the Maoz Israel Report every month, also free of charge! This is one of the most reputable Messianic publications coming out of Israel.

IN THE RIGHT HANDS, THIS BOOK WILL CHANGE LIVES!

Most of the people who need this message will not be looking for this book. To change their lives, you need to put a copy of this book in their hands.

> *But others (seeds) fell into good ground, and brought forth fruit, some a hundred-fold, some sixty-fold, some thirty-fold* (Matthew 13:8).

Our ministry is constantly seeking methods to find the good ground, the people who need this anointed message to change their lives. Will you help us reach these people?

> *Remember this—a farmer who plants only a few seeds will get a small crop. But the one who plants generously will get a generous crop* (2 Corinthians 9:6).

EXTEND THIS MINISTRY BY SOWING
3 BOOKS, 5 BOOKS, 10 BOOKS, OR MORE TODAY,
AND BECOME A LIFE CHANGER!

Thank you,

Don Nori Sr., Founder
Destiny Image
Since 1982